Night Shift in Barcelona

Welcome to Santa Aelina University Hospital…

As night falls on Barcelona's busiest hospital, its bustling wards transform… From the hush-filled NICU to the tense operating theater, the Spanish city might be fast asleep, but St. Aelina's night shift team are *always* on standby for their patients—and each other! And in the heat of the Mediterranean night, that mix of drama and dedication might hand the hardworking staff a chance at summer love!

Set your alarm and join the night shift with…

The Night They Never Forgot by Scarlet Wilson

Their Barcelona Baby Bombshell by Traci Douglass

Their Marriage Worth Fighting For by Louisa Heaton

From Wedding Guest to Bride? by Tina Beckett

Dear Reader,

Every once in a while a story comes along that does a number on my heart. When the story line for my contribution to the Night Shift in Barcelona continuity arrived in my inbox, I knew this was going to be just such a story.

Like the heroine in my book, I was seriously injured in a riding accident when my horse stumbled unexpectedly. I fractured a vertebra in my lower back and faced the prospect of surgery to stabilize my spine. Unlike the heroine in *From Wedding Guest to Bride?*, however, my spinal cord was intact. Another similarity is that I have been involved in an equine-assisted therapy program for a number of years. It is something I'm passionate about and something that makes a difference in people's lives.

So I hope as you escape into Santiago and Elena's story, you are transported into a world of uncertainty, but more importantly, a world of hope. Where anything is possible. Including love. And in the end, that's what matters most for these two amazing characters. Enjoy!

Love,

Tina Beckett

FROM WEDDING GUEST TO BRIDE?

TINA BECKETT

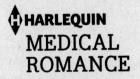

Special thanks and acknowledgment are given to Tina Beckett for
her contribution to the Night Shift in Barcelona miniseries.

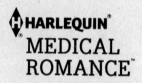

HARLEQUIN®
MEDICAL
ROMANCE™

Recycling programs
for this product may
not exist in your area.

ISBN-13: 978-1-335-73727-4

From Wedding Guest to Bride?

Copyright © 2022 by Harlequin Enterprises ULC

For questions and comments about the quality of this book,
please contact us at CustomerService@Harlequin.com.

Harlequin Enterprises ULC
22 Adelaide St. West, 41st Floor
Toronto, Ontario M5H 4E3, Canada
www.Harlequin.com

Printed in U.S.A.

Three-time Golden Heart® Award finalist **Tina Beckett** learned to pack her suitcases almost before she learned to read. Born to a military family, she has lived in the United States, Puerto Rico, Portugal and Brazil. In addition to traveling, Tina loves to cuddle with her pug, Alex, spend time with her family and hit the trails on her horse. Learn more about Tina from her website, or friend her on Facebook.

Books by Tina Beckett

Harlequin Medical Romance

The Island Clinic collection

How to Win the Surgeon's Heart

New York Bachelor's Club

Consequences of Their New York Night
The Trouble with the Tempting Doc

A Summer in São Paulo

One Hot Night with Dr. Cardoza

Miracle Baby for the Midwife
Risking It All for the Children's Doc
It Started with a Winter Kiss
Starting Over with the Single Dad
Their Reunion to Remember
One Night with the Sicilian Surgeon

Visit the Author Profile page
at Harlequin.com for more titles.

To those around the world who are involved in equine-assisted therapy.

PROLOGUE

THE GROUND WAS so much harder than Elena Solis remembered. She lay there, weird sounds emerging from her throat as she tried to draw a breath and failed. A bolt of panic surged through her. But despite all that, despite the continued gasp for air, despite her fear, she searched the area for her horse.

The music from the speakers at the boarding barn was still blaring, even though she and Stratosphere were no longer moving to the same beat.

It wasn't the first time she'd taken a hard fall. She'd pulled plenty of stupid stunts in her eighteen years, so she doubted it would be the last. Only this time, it wasn't a stunt. She'd been practicing for a show, the way she'd done hundreds of times before.

Her eyes arced over the space again, finding Sandra standing nearby.

"Don't worry. I have Strato. Are you okay? You hit pretty hard." Elena's closest friend had dismounted from her own horse and now held Strato's reins as well.

The poor boy had tripped as she'd rounded a corner during their freestyle routine, not an unheard-of occurrence. Thankfully he hadn't fallen on top of her. As always, she would just hop up and carry on. You had to get right back on after a fall, right? Wasn't that how the saying went? Except right now everything hurt. Her shoulder, her left knee.

But the worst was her back.

"Just give me a minute." She dragged in a shallow breath, then another, the tight band around her chest slowly easing, even as her pain levels crept higher.

She filled her lungs with air, eyes closing in relief that she could finally breathe normally again. Okay, now to get up. As she tried to roll onto her side, sudden shards of pain slashed at her back, and she felt a horrible burning sensation in her spine. Then nothing. Nothing at all. She immediately fell back and lay still, trying to think.

Okay, that had never happened before. The pain in her knee had vanished, though. That was a good thing. Right?

She wiggled her hands, her arms. Her toes.

Everything worked. Wait. Had her toes wiggled? She couldn't tell. She tried again. *Dios!*

"Sandra?" Her voice shook in a way it hadn't a moment ago.

Her friend took a step closer, the horses moving with her. Strato's head came down, and he nuzzled her shoulder, giving a soft nicker.

"Do you need a hand?" her friend asked.

"I—I don't know yet."

"What's wrong?" A hint of alarm had entered Sandra's voice.

"Can you look at my left foot?"

Her friend's attention moved downward. "What about it? Does it hurt?"

"Is it moving? Look at it. My left foot. *Is it moving?*"

"No, should it be?" Her friend's eyes met hers. "Elle? Talk to me. Are you in pain?"

Terror rose up and clogged Elena's throat, threatening to steal her breath all over again.

Her riding helmet pressed against the back of her skull. At least she'd worn that. "No, it doesn't hurt. And it should be moving. I'm telling it to move." *Please move! Please!* "Are you sure? Look again."

"Okay." Sandra's gaze flitted back toward her foot. "It's not doing anything. *Dios*, Elle, I think I need to call for help."

Elena swallowed, remaining very still, knowing she'd made a terrible mistake in trying to get up before she'd assessed the damage. How many times had her father warned her not to move someone who might have a back injury? "I think so, too. Because, for some reason… I—I can't feel my legs."

"Oh, Elle…" Her friend pulled out her cell phone and dialed.

Through a tunnel she heard Sandra telling someone where they were and what had happened and begging them to send help. Now.

All Elena could do, though, was lie there and pray. Pray harder than she'd ever done in her entire life.

CHAPTER ONE

Santiago Garcia had never seen his friend Caitlin look more radiant or more beautiful as she glided down the aisle to meet the man she called *el amor de mi vida*. The love of her life. Santi had once had one of those, too. But not anymore. And he'd never felt less festive about an event like this than he did right now. It was the first wedding he'd agreed to attend since Carmen's death had ripped his life apart six years ago. And right now, as he sat in a plush pew in the ornate estate chapel, he was sorry he'd come. But he'd traveled all the way to Andalusia from Barcelona, and to skip the wedding at the last second would have raised eyebrows. And Caitlin didn't deserve to have one second of her happiness affected by his behavior.

A slight movement to his left caught his attention. The woman seated next to him rearranged her skirt over her legs for the third time since she'd wheeled herself into her spot moments earlier.

She looked almost as unhappy to be here as he felt.

Without turning his head, he studied her out of the corner of his eye as a way of avoiding the joy that radiated from the front of the chapel. With raven-black hair that wound its way down her back, the woman sat proud and erect, her slender shoulders bared by a green slinky dress. The color was perfect against her smooth skin. She was stunning. And evidently alone. Just like him. Not that it made the slightest bit of difference.

Santi wasn't here to meet women. He was here to wish his friend well. Once that was done, he was free to return to Barcelona. Back to his life.

He forced his attention back to the front, more anxious than ever to get out of here.

Caitlin and her soon-to-be husband were holding hands and the officiant was instructing Javier to place a ring on Cait's finger. Their eyes met, and Javier leaned over to whisper something in Caitlin's ear. Something that made her lips curve.

Santi's muscles tightened in remembrance of doing that exact thing with Carmen. Whispering about how much he loved her. How he couldn't wait to walk down that aisle as husband and wife. Some strange impulse made him glance across, searching the fingers his neighbor had clasped in her lap. No ring. Not on any of her fingers.

Why had he just done that? It didn't matter if she was married or available. He'd taken off his ring a couple of years ago but had felt a vague twinge of guilt when he had, his empty finger whispering an accusation that wasn't true. Because *nothing* could make him forget his wife.

The woman next to him glanced his way without warning, making him jerk his gaze back to the front, where it belonged. But not before he saw the slight frown that furrowed her brow. He agreed with her. He'd had no business staring at her.

The rings were exchanged and vows repeated back to each other, and as the strident chords of the organ began to play, Javier bent over to kiss Caitlin on the lips, lingering there long enough for the guests to chuckle, a few whistles echoing off the formal walls, where stern saints seemed to chastise the interruption. Then the couple parted and turned to face the back of the chapel. Javier raised their clasped hands, kissing his bride's knuckles before they began their march down the aisle. Caitlin smiled at him as she went by. Or had it been at the mystery woman to his left? She was seated on the bride's side, so they had to know each other.

From where?

It didn't matter. Maybe she was a childhood friend, or someone from school.

As soon as Caitlin and Javier and their wedding party exited through the massive doors, the woman beside him whirled her chair around and disappeared into the crowd that now streamed toward the back. Anxious to get away from him?

Hell, why wouldn't she be? He'd stared at her for most of the ceremony, although most of that was out of avoidance.

Avoidance? Was that all it had been? The woman was beautiful. She probably had men staring at her all the time. Maybe that's why she'd seemed so irritated when she'd caught him in the act.

Well, he didn't need to worry about it. Once he got through the reception dinner, he was free to leave for his hotel. Or maybe he'd try to catch a flight straight back to Barcelona and his apartment, which was not far from Santa Aelina Hospital. The university hospital had been new when he'd been approached to come and be a part of it, and he'd jumped at the chance. He didn't regret the move. Even though he'd lost Carmen a year after moving to Barcelona.

He took his time making his way to the reception, which was held in one of the ballrooms of the huge estate. Sliding through the doors, he winced at the strands of white lights that were artfully draped throughout the space, giving it a sense of intimacy that made him balk at moving farther into the room. But the people coming up behind forced him to move away from the entry, deeper into the belly of the beast. The love and romance fairly pulsed through the space. And it was evidently contagious with people everywhere holding hands and murmuring to each other. The occasional outburst of laughter made him even more uncomfortable.

His eyes scanned the area, and it took a second before he realized what he was unconsciously searching for. The woman who'd sat beside him in the chapel. To apologize?

Maybe she'd think his staring was because she was in a wheelchair. But she'd be wrong. And trying to explain that seemed worse somehow. So he was going to let it go.

Besides, he didn't see her anywhere.

He went over to the bar, waiting in line for a drink. Anything was better than standing against the wall and watching the rest of the world enjoy themselves, while he tried to plug a hole that was spewing memories of Carmen like a broken water main. This was why he didn't do weddings. He'd toyed several times with returning to Argentina, but he didn't want to get his parents' hopes up that he would take over the family business. While he loved horses and polo—having grown up with them—that wasn't where his heart was.

Santi loved medicine. Loved being a pediatrician. Even more so now that his dreams of having a family of his own had been snatched away by the cruel hand of fate.

He ordered a Scotch on the rocks, taking a sip before stepping away from the bar. He savored the bite, the chill of the ice burrowing beneath the warmth of the liquor. It was a sensation he knew all too well. After Carmen's death, he had taken far too many slugs of room-temperature whisky over a period of months. He'd cut back before it had gotten completely out of hand, and he'd found the addition of ice made him slow down and think, rather than mindlessly toss back shot after shot.

A flash of green caught his eye before disappearing again. He squinted in that direction while taking another sip of his drink.

It probably wasn't even his mystery woman.

His?

No. She wasn't. And he had no intention of trying to change that.

Caitlin and Javier appeared in front of him. They must be making the rounds rather than standing in a reception line. He couldn't blame them.

"Thanks for coming, Santi. I wasn't sure you would."

He knew Caitlin and some of the rest of the staff at Santa Aelina's had been worried about him after Carmen's death. He'd refused to talk to anyone and had brooded in his office whenever he didn't have patients. He refused to go to any events not related to the hospital and had equally rebuffed Caitlin's mentions of going to the hospital's counseling center.

"I told you I would."

She smiled. "I know. And you always keep your promises, don't you." She leaned forward and kissed his cheek. "Well, I'm glad you're here. It means a lot to me."

Javier held his hand out, and Santi gripped it.

"Congratulations to you both. I'm happy for you."

The lie slipped out so easily that it sounded true. It wasn't that he *wasn't* happy for them. He just found it hard to bleed an emotion that no longer flowed through his veins. Nowadays, he found his fulfillment and purpose in his work. It filled his days with meaning, and right now, he couldn't ask for any more than that. Didn't really deserve any more than that.

His friend eyed him. "Sorry to talk shop right now, but there's a case I might ask you to look at when you get home, since we'll be gone on our honeymoon for a while. Teenage patient complaining of leg and foot pain."

"Tomás?" Javier glanced at Caitlin.

She nodded at her husband before looking back at Santi. "He was born with hypoplastic left heart syndrome."

Santi frowned. HLHS was a congenital malformation of the heart where only half of it was capable of pumping blood. It was normally a death sentence. "And he's a teenager?"

"He had the Fontan procedure as a child and has done remarkably well with it."

He didn't understand where he came in. Fontan circulation was a complicated rerouting of the heart vessels that helped bypass unusable portions of the organ. It was a delicate balance, since cardiac output never became what was considered "normal."

"You're both cardiologists, and I'm a pediatrician, so I'm not sure how I can help."

Javier inserted, "We've basically ruled out

the pain being caused by the circulatory system itself. We've talked about bringing you in, there's just been no time—"

"You helped me with a case a few weeks ago, remember, Santi? And there's a new doctor coming on board—a diagnostician. I think I mentioned her to you before. She's already said she'll examine him." She squeezed his arm. "Anyway, look at his chart and see what you think. His name is Tomás Lopez."

"Okay, I will." He hadn't needed to contact the diagnostician last time as he'd solved the issue himself. He welcomed complex cases. They used brain cells that might otherwise be occupied with things he couldn't change. And what was the worst that could happen? The new diagnostician telling him to mind his own business? If she did, she did. He no longer worried much about stepping on toes.

Caitlin hugged him. "Thanks. Keep me updated."

Her husband shot her a look that made her grin.

"Okay, I know I promised no work on our honeymoon. But I'd like to know what they find."

Javier tipped her chin and planted a kiss on it. "I'm kidding. I want to know, too."

With that, the happy couple turned to speak with the person on his right.

Blowing out a breath, he took another drink and found that too much ice had melted during their conversation, taking the bite out of the Scotch. Setting the remainder of his drink on a tray designated for discarded glasses, he forced his mind to work through what little information Caitlin and Javier had given him.

The sound of a spoon rhythmically tapping against a wineglass broke through the chatter, and more people joined in until it became a solid clanging wall of sound. Folks moved to sit at the large round tables where food would soon be served.

Santi knew what was coming. Before Javier kissed Caitlin to appease the crowd, or the first person had a chance to propose a toast to the happy couple, he slipped out of the room.

Shoving his hands into the pockets of his dress pants, he wandered down the hallway, the quiet click of his shoes on the tile a marked contrast to the noise of all those people in the ballroom. At last he could hear himself think, although that could be a double-edged sword.

An open door to his right caught his attention and he peeked inside and saw a huge area of shelves lined with books. A library. Perfect. He could find a quiet corner and sit for a while. He didn't dare leave quite yet, when his absence might be noted.

Ducking inside, he made his way over to look at a tile mural tucked between two of the bookshelves. He studied it, giving a snort at what the scene depicted. A couple dressed in ornate period clothing sat astride a galloping horse. Not only were they sitting, they were, in fact, sidesaddle. Both of them. The couple kissed, the draped reins flapping uselessly against the steed's neck as it raced across the countryside. Evidently romance trumped reality everywhere, not just in the chapel.

"Seriously?" he muttered.

"I thought the same."

The soft words came from somewhere behind him. He closed his eyes as he realized he wasn't alone. He certainly hadn't meant for anyone to hear him scorning the local decor. Especially since the painter was probably someone famous.

Well, at least it sounded like the person agreed with him. So maybe someone besides a horse person could spot how ludicrous the scene was.

Well, even a wedding contained ridiculous promises of forever, didn't it? No one knew what the future held. And no one knew that more than he did. So why had those wedding vows not changed to any large degree over the last couple of centuries? Plagues, pestilence, wars…cancer. Any one of them had the power to grind those promises into dust.

Realizing he was still standing there in the same position he'd been moments earlier, and probably seeming very rude to whomever had spoken to him, he slowly turned around, trying to explain as he did.

"Sorry, it's just that I was raised on a—"

His words faltered for a second before dying away completely.

The flash of green he'd spotted in the ballroom… It was repeated here. What the hell were the odds of that?

The faint sounds of laughter carried in from the ballroom, and he tensed before he realized his focus was fixed on the mystery woman.

He was staring at her just like he'd done in the chapel less than an hour earlier. He blinked and forced his eyes to move away before looking at her again.

"It's you."

As soon as the words were out of his mouth, he felt a swell of irritation wash over him. He'd sounded shocked. And pleased.

And the last thing he wanted was to sound like a breathless teenager.

Her quick smile wiped away his irritation as her brows went up in question.

"Yes. It's me. Although I'm not sure what you mean by that. Should I be flattered or insulted?"

Elle was good at hiding her feelings. So she hoped the sense of shock had been veiled beneath an air of lazy amusement. When the man had wandered into the library, she hadn't realized who he was at first. But the sound of disbelief when he'd gone over to the picture had made her smile. The impulse to glide away on silent wheels had come and gone as curiosity made her sit there and see what he would do or say next.

She'd come here to get away from the crush of people in the ballroom. Crowds gave her a strange sense of claustrophobia as they towered over her. At times, she felt invisible, which she knew wasn't what anyone intended, and there wasn't much they could do about it, other than sit down.

So observing this one man as he studied the mural was much more interesting than going back into the reception. She probably knew a few of the people there, although she hadn't really seen anyone besides the bride and groom.

But when he'd turned around and she recognized him as the man who'd sat next to her in the chapel, shock had shot through her. It was evidently the same for him, judging by his words.

His mouth twitched. "Sorry. I thought I was alone. It seems you've seen my bad side twice now."

"Twice?" She had no idea what he was talking about.

"Never mind. I just needed to get away for a minute and then I saw…" He motioned back toward the mural. "Did the painter never once throw a leg over a horse?"

She blinked, eyes going wide. "I haven't heard that expression in a while. You ride?"

"I haven't recently, but I used to quite a lot."

"So did I." She expected to see disbelief go through his eyes, but there was nothing.

Nothing…except something she wasn't quite sure of.

He came over and took a seat in one of the gilt chairs in front of her and smiled. "Okay, so tell me. Have you ever ridden bareback while kissing someone—as your horse charged across a field? And actually stayed seated?"

She flinched as she remembered her fall all those years ago, but quickly covered by saying, "Nope, I've never done that. Never even wanted to do that. You?"

He laughed, glancing back. "You mean you don't recognize me in that painting?"

Her answering laugh took her by surprise. He was talking to her as if she could do anything. People often tiptoed around her, being careful with what they said, afraid they would hurt her feelings. They didn't realize that very act hurt. Even the few dates she'd gone on had been full of men rushing to do things for her that she could do for herself. After a particularly disastrous encounter, she finally decided she didn't need a life partner. They were just too much work, and she was pretty sure they thought the same thing about her. Her college professor being one of them.

"Well, I thought you looked vaguely familiar."

There was suddenly a sense of relief about him that she wondered about. He'd seemed so ill at ease seated beside her in the chapel, and she'd thought maybe it had to do with her chair, but there was none of that now. It had been embarrassing, because what she'd noticed first and foremost about him was that he was a man. A very, very attractive man.

And hearing him talk… *Dios*, his voice only increased that awareness. His voice had a low gravelly quality that caught at her insides and made them quiver. All the way to the middle of her left thigh, which was the lowest part of her body that had retained sensation. Her injury hadn't completely severed her spinal cord. And the parts that could still feel had the ability to detect the most minute sensations. The lightest brush against her skin. So the pleasure of his voice...

Oh, man, it was nice. More than nice.

She cleared her throat. "Anyway, you can kind of see why the painter concentrated on the couple rather than the horse in that mural. After all, Caitlin and Javier only had eyes for each other during the ceremony."

"Yes. I guess that's true."

The words were said in that same gruff intonation as before, but it was as if a shutter had suddenly slammed down in his eyes. The uneasiness had returned as he leaned back in his chair, arms going across his chest.

Okay, so this was a subject that was touchy with him for some reason. It didn't take a diagnostician to read his body language. She could have done it with no medical degree at all.

He wasn't angry. More like he was putting up a roadblock that read "Closed to through traffic."

She could understand that. There were still areas of her life that she didn't talk about with just anyone. But she mourned the loss of the playful conversation they'd had just minutes earlier. All because of a careless comment.

But how could she have known?

She reached for the books she'd found when she'd first come into the library, hoping to recreate the ease between them. "Do you know much about the history of the Maravilla estate? It's kind of fascinating actually."

She stumbled through a couple of more sentences about the house and grounds before taking a breath. And in that time there was a silence that made her teeth clench.

This was why she didn't talk about stuff like this. Her fixation on the smallest details didn't sit well with most people. She waited for his eyes to glaze over and for him to make an excuse to leave.

Only she didn't want him to leave. Not just yet. And she wasn't sure why.

Surprise washed through her when neither of those things happened. Instead, his arms uncrossed, and he leaned forward. "I don't actually know anything about it."

"Oh, really?" Her eyes met his, and she

swallowed, fumbling with the book she'd grabbed. She flipped to the first page that had a picture. It was the one from the mural on the wall. "Oh! Well…"

The man chuckled. A warm sound that made a rush of pleasure run through her. This man could be very dangerous. "You planned that didn't you?"

"I didn't. Honest." But her words came out breathy with a strange huskiness that wasn't familiar.

She recognized the attraction for what it was and knew it was risky to continue down this path. But somehow, she didn't want to exit the conversation. Wanted to see what would happen if she stayed here and let things take their course.

His gaze locked on her face, shifting subtly to her mouth and pausing there. It knocked the breath from her lungs.

"Didn't you?"

A buzzing started up in her head as he continued to look at her. Her tongue flicked out to moisten her lips, and she watched him capture the movement before forcing herself to answer him.

"Why would I do that? You don't even like that mural."

"The mural? Hmm… No. I'm not impressed by that."

Said as if he was impressed by something else, instead.

Her? Surely not. But what if…?

How long had it been since she'd engaged in back-and-forth banter like this? It could almost be considered flirting, couldn't it?

And was she? Flirting?

Yes. She thought she was. She was never going to see the man after tonight, so what was the harm?

Against her volition, her back curved, as if something in him was pulling her toward him. Some magnetic force. Her hands went to her knees, pushing slightly to keep herself balanced in her chair.

The chair was the only place she was balanced. Her mind, her heart, her body… They were all rocking on some sort of precipice. One tiny push and…

"So what impresses you?" She couldn't believe she'd just asked that. And yet she didn't want to retract the question.

"All kinds of things. This country. This

place." There was a slight pause before he continued. "And you."

She realized they were now inches away. The buzzing in her head spread to her body, until her entire being vibrated with a strange kind of urgency.

She recognized it a second before warm fingertips touched her cheek, sliding down it until he reached the corner of her mouth and cupped her chin. Tilting it up. Her pulse skyrocketed, and everything in her willed him to do it. Wanted him to do it.

"Yes," he murmured. "Most definitely you."

And then he leaned forward and did exactly what she'd been waiting for. He pressed his lips to hers.

CHAPTER TWO

SOMEWHERE IN THE back of his mind, he heard something clatter to the floor.

The book.

Except that's not what he wanted to think about right now. Not with this woman's sweet mouth pressed against his. And instead of moving away, she was inching closer.

Her hands curved around his shoulders. Maybe it was to help support herself, but the sudden touch rocketed through him like a missile, sending all kinds of crazy thoughts pumping through him. It was insane and heady and he never wanted it to end.

Her warm fingers toyed with the hair at his nape and a rush of need pumped through his body, making him want things he hadn't wanted in what seemed like forever. Things like intimacy. Sharing.

Caring.

Things he hadn't wanted since…

Carmen.

He sat back in a hurry before he realized he was dragging her with him. Reaching out to steady her and help her regain her balance, he ground his teeth together. Hell, what had he been playing at?

Diablos! Kissing her made as much sense as the scene in that damned mural!

He didn't even know this person, yet he'd been locked in an embrace that he almost hadn't been able to break. If not for…

"*Santo Dios.* I'm sorry."

Up went her chin. "Don't be. It was just a kiss. It meant nothing."

She smiled, but there was a brittle edge to it. She'd gone from soft and warm and so passionate it had made his blood heat, to a state that was chillier than those cubes of ice in his drink a half hour earlier. Only there was nothing watered down about this. And her words were sharp and biting and filled with an anger he didn't understand.

He shouldn't have kissed her. And now she wanted him to leave. That much he understood. So he climbed to his feet, staring down at her for a few seconds trying to find a different way to apologize, one that would make for a softer exit. But he found nothing. No words that would work in a situation like this. Not that he'd ever been in one.

It meant nothing.

Hell, he wished that were true. And maybe for her it was. But for him…?

What they'd shared a moment ago was the first time he'd felt out of control since his wife's death. Other than two quick encounters with other women, he'd pretty much been celibate. And he preferred it that way.

And this? Well, this was the first real kiss he'd had since that time. The first kiss with no end goal in sight. He'd kissed her simply because he'd wanted to. And that fact just made the guilt rise higher. He knew he wasn't betraying Carmen, but it sure as hell felt like he was.

The woman's head was bent, and she stared at the splayed hands in her lap. He didn't want to leave her like this, wanted to at least ask her what her name was. But he didn't think she'd welcome anything he might say right now. So with one last look, he turned and walked away.

Away from her. And most of all, away from that damned mural on the wall.

"Elle?"

She'd zoned out again. For the third time, since her friend and mentor, Letizia Morgado, started showing her around Santa Aelina Hospital. And it all centered on that surreal experience at the Maravilla estate. It had almost been like a scene out of *Cinderella*. Only the man had been no prince. And Elena was no downtrodden stepsister. But that kiss... As short as it had been, its memory still had the power to send shivers of need through her.

And she didn't like it.

"Sorry."

"Are you okay with this? Staying in one place? Caitlin said you were but..." Her friend's worried glance said volumes.

Elle had preferred to travel from hospital to hospital, justifying it with the idea that she could learn more and be better at what she did by having a wide range of experiences. But maybe the truth was that she'd had a hard time trusting people since her accident. The world had turned into a dark and scary place for a few years after her fall, and some of her friends had silently slid away, including her high school boyfriend, who'd sent excuses for why he stopped coming to visit her in the hospital.

Sandra was one of the few who hadn't deserted her. And Strato now resided with her at her home on the island of Mallorca. Elle had retired him after her accident, not able to bear the thought of selling him and not knowing what might happen to him down the line. She was happy knowing he was loved and cared for, even if she hadn't been out to visit him in the last three years.

"I'm sure. Caitlin has a case she wants me to look at. Besides, you've done a wonderful job with accessibility at the hospital. We haven't been one place where I had trouble getting around."

Letizia smiled. "Thanks. It was a hard battle, just like it is everywhere. It's not that people don't want accessibility. It's just something they don't always think about. This hospital really wanted to work on that." Her friend spun to face her. Their wheelchairs were as unique as their personalities. Letizia's green spiked hair and the bold stickers plastered all over her transportation were in stark contrast to Elena's sleek chair that was built for maneuverability and comfort. Elle also had a racing chair at home that she'd used for various walk, roll or run marathons.

"A new case. I heard about that. Must be interesting if Caitlin is asking for another set of eyes."

"I know. I'll look at the patient's chart as soon as I get to wherever you guys are putting me. Fifth floor, right? In the research and teaching departments?"

"Actually, if you're okay with it, we have an office on this floor you can use while working this particular case. You may be shuffled around the hospital a bit when there's a complicated case to make it easier for you, but you're right, your 'home' department will be up on the fifth."

She smiled. "Well, see there? I'll still be moving from place to place. It'll just all be in the same building." Actually that made her feel better. If she bounced from one department to another, she wouldn't get that claustrophobic sense of panic that she'd had her last year of high school when everything had changed. She still got that whenever she was in one place for too long. It was irrational, and she'd done her best to combat it, but it was still there. That fear had chased her away from any relationships she'd had since her accident. You never knew when life could change completely. But if she just could stay ahead of it…if she could just outrun it—or out roll it, in her case—she would be fine. She hoped.

Letizia headed toward the end of the hallway, pushing a button to open a door on the right. "Okay, then. This will be your office, for now."

Elle moved past her, eyes widening as she took in the large space. "Are you sure this is the right place?"

In the back of the office, there was a huge window that looked out over Aelina Park, the green space the hospital had put in as the facility was being built. With a tree-planting program and dirt paths made for walking or jogging, the park spanned the space between the hospital and the staff quarters just beyond. She couldn't wait to take her other chair out on that path and get back to her workouts. There was also a little man-made creek that ran along part of the trail that was stocked with fish and could be enjoyed by birds and small wildlife. It was beautiful. And peaceful. Something that really resonated with Elle, who desperately needed that peace.

"This is it. Caitlin requested it especially for you. It'll make it easier for you and Dr. Garcia to work on the case."

Dr. Garcia must be the pediatrician her friend had told her about. She just hoped the person didn't get his feathers ruffled, the way some doctors did if she didn't kowtow to their every thought.

Maybe that's why she had this space. For meetings about their patient. There was a table with four chairs and a plush sofa that looked like it might pull into a bed.

Okay, she could get a little too used to this. "Well, thanks. I'll take good care of it. While I'm here, anyway."

"Are you planning to leave again? I hope not."

Elle hesitated. "No. I just meant while I'm using the office." Had her words contained a hidden meaning? Was she thinking of her stay at Santa Aelina's as being temporary?

No. She needed to overcome some of her hang-ups, and this was the perfect time and place. She rolled over to the desk and reached behind her for the backpack that contained her laptop and some items for her workspace. Setting it on the light wood surface, she glanced again at the park.

Letizia must have seen her look. "Did you get into your apartment yet?"

"Yes. I think it will work out perfectly. Do most of the staff live there?"

"Some of us do. But not everyone. Those who live farther out normally either take the bus or ride bikes—another way Santa Aelina's is different."

"I noticed the bike racks near the main entrance."

"Yep. That reminds me." She went behind the desk, motioning Elle to follow her. "The outlets that are blue have electricity supplied by solar panels on the roof on the west side of the building. We try to plug phone chargers and computers into those to cut our power consumption."

"I'm impressed. Thanks for letting me know."

"You're welcome. And I'd better head

back to work myself. Let me know if you're free for lunch anytime soon."

"I will. For now, I just want to grab the notes on this case and get up to speed before Dr. Garcia wants to meet."

"All right, *querida*, I'll let you get to it, then."

Elle smiled at the endearment. She might not have a ton of friends—by choice—but she loved the ones she did have. "See you."

Letizia closed the door behind her, leaving her to get set up in the office. Opening the backpack, she pulled out her pencil cup, laptop and a picture of her family, hesitating over the snapshot of her with Strato, pre-accident. She'd thrown it into her pack at the last minute. But it might bring up a lot of questions she wouldn't necessarily want to answer. So maybe she would hold on to it until she started using her space on the fifth floor.

Zipping her backpack up again, she managed to drag the chair out and away from the desk so she could park her wheelchair there. She shifted the weight off her left hip and seat bone. She was fortunate to still have feeling in part of that leg, but the price had been a form of neuralgia that ranged from a dull ache to a sharp pins-and-needles sensation at times.

She plugged her charger and laptop into the plug Letizia had indicated and popped open the top of her computer. Pulling her access code out of her purse, she linked into the hospital's system and found her patient. His name was Tomás Lopez.

"Okay." The file was long. She scrolled trying to find the end of it but gave up. Instead she sorted the case file by dates and came to the most recent entries that included a long list of symptoms. "Okay, here we go."

She'd been staring at the screen for about five minutes when a knock sounded at her door. "Come in." Not wanting to lose her place, it took her a minute to look up.

Shock swung through her like an ax, severing whatever concentration she'd had minutes earlier.

It was The Kiss! Er…the man. The one from the wedding. Oh, God! Why hadn't Caitlin warned her?

Because her other friend had no idea what had transpired in that library. And even if she had, she'd probably have been urging her to explore the possibilities.

There were no possibilities.

Maybe this wasn't even Dr. Garcia. *Dios*, she hoped not.

The man finished coming into the office, the dismay on his face obvious. He was just as shocked as she was. He frowned, a heavy furrowing of brows that made her cringe.

"I'm sorry," he finally said. "I'm looking for Dr. Solis."

She couldn't stop a laugh. Of course he was. Because that's just the way her luck ran. Or maybe she should say the opposite of luck.

"That would be me."

"Diablos."

The swear word was almost too low for her to hear but hear it she did. She also saw the muscle that worked in his cheek for a minute. In a voice that was a little gruffer, he continued. "Why didn't you say something at the wedding about working at the hospital?"

A familiar tingle went through her abdomen. One she was quick to suppress.

"I'm sorry? Was I *supposed* to say something?"

"Did Caitlin tell you who I was?"

"Nope. I had no idea. If I had…" If she had, she would have what? Not let him kiss her? And missed the best kiss ever? Somehow she didn't want to wish that away, so she submerged it instead.

"Yeah. Me, too." The words were said with a sense of quiet…regret.

So she might not regret what had happened in that room, but he did. It was obvious in the stiff way he held himself. In his reaction when he realized exactly who she was.

It made a thread of anger go through her. It was okay to lock lips with her as long as he never had to run across her path again?

To be fair, wasn't that what she had thought as well? That it was something she could look back on with…what? Fondness? Maybe. As if they'd been at a masquerade party, had flirted with each other, but never removed their masks and revealed their identities. It was titillating in some weird way.

Whatever it was, she didn't want to erase it.

But what was happening right now was not titillating. Or exciting. And it definitely wasn't comfortable.

Her lips twisted as she tried to think of something to say, before grabbing at the first thing that slid through her mind. "We can't take back what happened. So let's just put it behind us and move forward." She reached out her hand. "Elena Solis. But you can call me Elle. Most people do."

He grasped her hand. "Santiago Garcia. Santi."

Santi. One letter away from being a saint. Only this man was no *santo*. Saints didn't kiss like that.

"I take it you and I will be working together. At least for this one case."

"That's what Caitlin said. She and Javier have exhausted all cardiac issues as being the cause of Tomás's symptoms."

"Which are? I just started looking at his file, can you fill me in?"

"Sure. He's been having leg and foot pain for the last three months or so. It's been steadily getting worse. They thought at first it might be due to a lack of perfusion caused by the Fontan procedure, but—"

"Wait. Back up. I haven't heard most of this. What tests were run? How did they rule out circulatory issues?"

Dr. Garcia didn't have to look at notes, he just went through Tomás's diagnosis at birth straight through to where things stood now. She was surprised by the details he remembered. That had always been something she prided herself on, her memory. It looked like the pediatrician's was every bit as good if not better than hers.

Not that any of that mattered right now.

"And there were no issues with his feet or legs until now."

"No. They thought maybe he was getting ready to go through a growth spurt or puberty, which I'm sure you know is sometimes delayed in Fontan circulation patients. He's also near the bottom of the growth chart for his age."

"Liver? Kidneys?"

"Nothing outside of what would be expected in a case like his. Enzymes are no more elevated than they have been in the past. His circulatory system is as stable as it can be, although it will never be normal without a heart transplant. He'll go on the transplant list if something changes."

"Okay, thanks. So other causes? Growth plate pain?"

"Caitlin said they thought of that and had one of Santa Aelina's orthopedists look at the X-rays. Nothing showed up. And the pain is only in a section running from his thighs all the way down to and including his feet."

She shifted again at the memory of her own transient pain. "Neuralgia?"

"It's on my list of differentials. But I want to run through all the possibilities before just slapping a label on it."

She smiled. "I totally agree with that." She'd had enough labels slapped on her to last a lifetime. And medical opinions were sometimes a dime a dozen. Her parents had taken her to a long list of specialists, some of whom said she'd never regain any sensation and others who claimed they'd be able to make her walk again. But she also knew how it felt to be poked and prodded until you were ready to scream. There was a balance there between the oath to do no harm and the pain they had to cause to help with the healing process. "Can we go see him?"

"Yes, that's why I came over. I was getting ready to go meet him and wondered if you were at a place where you could join me. Caitlin said he's not been the most cooperative of patients." He paused. "He's in the system."

"System?" As in a juvenile offender?

"No. More like his latest in a long line of *padres de acogida* who've turned him back over to the group home he was living in."

Foster parents. Her heart ached. "And his biological parents?"

"Single mother who couldn't handle the special needs baby who'd been born to her. Not and continue to work and care for her other children."

"I see." So this child had no one, other than the government…and his doctors. "I definitely want to go see him."

She hoped Santi hadn't seen the flash of compassion that went through her when he'd told her about Tomás's situation. As much as she tried to maintain a professional distance, it wasn't always easy. That went for this doctor evidently, too, because she'd caught the way his eyes quickly went over her when he'd sat down to talk to her. Suddenly she was wishing she'd worn something snazzier than her gauzy navy blouse and cream pants.

Was she trying to impress him? No. Absolutely not.

Their wordplay from the library at Maravilla came back to her in an instant, threatening to hijack her thoughts.

She quickly brought them back under control. "Shall we go?"

"Sure." He waited for her to get her phone and backpack, slinging the latter over the handle of her chair before she exited and hurried away from Santi…from her weird awareness of him.

"He's around the corner, the last doorway on the right."

"Okay, thanks."

He moved to walk beside her. "Any thoughts on where to start?"

"I want to see him, first, before I even start to speculate. Things like, is there any weakness accompanying the pain? Is the area of pain expanding? Contracting?"

He nodded. "Yes, it's hard to just read a case file and come up with a plan, although that seems to be how the game is played at times."

"I don't think of it as a game, but I remember being frustrated by that in med school. How were we supposed to come up with a differential diagnosis from a set of words put to paper?"

He smiled. "So I wasn't the only one who thought that."

Elena hadn't even wondered about it until she'd met her first patient and realized how different it was to hear someone describe in their own words what was going on with their body. She could remember when she was injured and doctors made pronouncements that hadn't resonated with her. At the time, she'd been too young and scared to challenge anyone. But now that she was a doctor herself, she found she wanted her patients' input, although there had certainly been times when a colleague from another hospital had sent her a case file and asked her opinion. So it wasn't that she couldn't work that way. She just preferred not to.

She also preferred not to work with someone she'd once kissed. She'd gone out and slept with one of her professors from medical school—after she'd graduated, of course—which was an unmitigated disaster. One that had never been repeated. And one-night stands were not for her.

So she wouldn't have slept with Dr. Garcia, given the chance that night at the wedding? She had a feeling she might have, breaking one of her self-imposed rules.

There. The door to their patient's room. Time to stop thinking about things she couldn't change.

Santi knocked and a second later entered the room holding the door for her.

"Hi, Tomás. I'm Dr. Garcia and this is Dr. Solis. We're here to check on you and see if we can figure out a way to help you."

The boy on the bed, who was probably fourteen or fifteen, lifted his shoulder in a shrug as if he couldn't care less who they were. But surely that was all for show. His notes had described his pain as a seven or eight at its worst and a five on good days.

Elena maneuvered so she was closer to the bed, but far enough away to allow him to have some personal space. "I've been reading your chart. Can you tell me when you first started to have pain?"

His chin jerked up. "I thought you said you read it. So you should already know."

She smiled, not put off by his abrupt manner. "I did, but I'd like to hear it in your own words."

Tomás shrugged again. "Don't know. My legs hurt. That's all I can tell you."

Okay, so he wasn't going to make this easy on them. That was okay. Because she didn't need "easy" to do her job. "Let's start with an easier question, then. What is your pain level right now?"

He jabbed his thumb at a picture on the wall as if he'd done it thousands of times. "Frowny face guy."

The pain level chart had both a set of numerical indicators and faces depicting different expressions.

His description made her smile. "So, *fuerte*. How long have you been in this much pain?"

"Since you guys arrived. Maybe you should just leave me alone."

She laughed. "I assume you're talking about Dr. Garcia's arrival and not mine." She shot the other doctor a grin.

"I was about to say the very same thing."

Santi sat on the chair next to her. "We will need to examine you, though, Tomás. Seriously. The sooner we figure this thing out, the sooner you'll get out of here."

His chin went up and he fixed them with a glare. "You mean leave the hospital?"

The pediatrician nodded. "Yep. I know you must be looking forward to that."

The boy's expression underwent a subtle shift that made something in her stomach churn. His cloak of anger seemed to lift for just a brief second before his eyes went hard all over again.

"Well, then, you don't know anything. Because I don't want to leave."

CHAPTER THREE

I DON'T WANT to leave.

He'd said it with as much surliness as Santi had ever heard, but what was he hiding underneath that? How much emotional pain would it take to make staying at a hospital preferable to wherever he would go after he was discharged?

He'd watched Elena's face contort at the words before getting herself back under control. Who could blame her? This boy's case was one of the most heartbreaking things he'd heard since becoming a pediatrician.

Who knew how many people had let this boy down. Including his latest foster parents. He pushed back the sympathy that threatened to interfere with his objectivity.

"The only way things are going to get better is if you let us help you."

"Who says they'll even get better? Maybe I'll just be stuck in a..." His glance snaked over to Elena, and he nodded at her. Santi was pretty sure he knew where the teen had been headed with his comment. But to let Tomás use his anger as a weapon to hurt someone else? No way. But before he could intervene, Elena spoke up instead.

"If you are, then you'll deal with it. You'll have no choice but to deal with it." Her soft voice came through, not hurling angry words back at the teen, but just being firm and matter-of-fact. "But you're not there. So let's see if we can find an answer. Help us do that."

The compassion he'd seen a second ago in her face was there in her words. And suddenly, Santi wanted to find an answer just as badly. Not because he didn't want Tomás to wind up in a wheelchair, but because he wanted to keep whatever was happening from progressing any further than it already had. Wanted to be someone this boy could trust.

He glanced at Elena. Her hair was pulled up in a long sleek ponytail today and her toenails were painted a light pink, something he hadn't noticed at the wedding due to her long dress. Her fingertips boasted no color, but those long, slender digits had propelled her down the hallway as if she'd done it her whole life. And maybe she had. Not something he was going to ask.

But if anyone knew what was at stake here, she did.

"So I'll ask again. Is it okay if we examine you?" Santi watched the boy's face.

Tomás shrugged. "Whatever. You gotta do what you gotta do, *tío*."

The kid was calling him *dude*? Really? Frustration sprouted all over again. He didn't like wasting his time. He was looking at this case as a favor to Caitlin. She'd said the boy was prickly. But that was putting it mildly. If he wasn't going to share anything outside of what was on the case notes, then this was a useless endeavor.

Santi leaned forward. "Listen…*tío*…" He purposely used the same term Tomás had used. "It's no hardship on me if you don't want to tell me what I need to know. I'll just call Dr. McKenzie and tell her that you evidently don't want to get better." He wasn't going to do any such thing. Caitlin deserved her happiness and he wouldn't do anything to upset her.

"Yeah, well *she* left me, too."

The words were a punch to Santi's gut. He could see how it might appear that way to this kid. He'd been left time and time again. "No. She got married. And she's very concerned about you. So is Dr. Torres. That's why we're here."

"And if you can't figure it out, either?"

Elena pushed a lock of hair off her face. "You're not giving us much to work with, though, are you?"

The teen crossed thin arms over his chest. "Fine. I was reaching across the dinner table one night to get another piece of meat and my *padre* yelled at me for being rude. I suddenly felt something hurt in both of my legs and screamed, clutching them." He stared at Santi and then Elena. "You know what he did? He claimed I was making it all up. He even told Dr. McKenzie that. Said I was doing it to get attention. So I agreed with him and went to my room. And the next day when they hurt again, I didn't say a word. I wasn't going to give him the satisfaction."

"What were you doing when they hurt the second time?" Santi asked.

Tomás looked at him as if trying to judge whether he really wanted to know or if he thought the illness was feigned as well. Santi knew better. A kid like this didn't use weakness to get attention. They made themselves as large and scary as possible. Just like he was doing here in this room.

"I was sitting on the bed and bent over to get my shoes off the floor."

Tomás's eyes came up and he pointed at his legs. "Just so you know, he was wrong. I wasn't making it up then, and I'm not making it up now."

"I believe you. So do some other people. That's why you're here now. Do your legs hurt all the time now?"

"Pretty much."

Santi stood. "I'd like to examine you now. Would that be okay?"

"I can't stop you."

"Yes, you can. All you have to do is say the word, and we'll leave."

Elena shot him a glance but didn't contradict him. Santi knew he was taking a risk, but he had to believe the boy didn't want to just sit in this room and let things play out. He and the diagnostician needed to keep on tackling this problem, one point at a time.

Another shrug. "Whatever. Go ahead."

"So yes?"

Tomás head gave a jerky nod, which he took as permission. Going to the side of the bed, he reached in his pocket for his stethoscope, looping it around his neck.

"Don't bother. My heart doesn't sound like other hearts."

"That's fine. I wasn't going to listen for that. I'm going to use it to listen to your belly and your lungs. But first I'm going to turn your head and bend your neck. Tell me if anything hurts."

He felt Elena's eyes on him and Tomás as he manipulated the boy's neck, turning it this way and that. "Does any of that hurt or make your legs hurt?"

The kid gave a harsh laugh. "My legs already hurt."

"Does it make them hurt worse?"

"No."

The one-word answer was evidently all he was going to get. He moved in front of him and stood just out of reach. "See if you can take my hands."

Tomás rolled his eyes, but did as he was asked, stretching his arms toward him, even as Santi took another step back. "Keep reaching."

"I can't."

"Humor me and try."

As he bent forward slightly, Tomás's face contorted. "Yeah, that hurts."

"Where?"

"My legs. And my stupid head."

Santi went very still as he mulled this piece of information. "Okay, you can relax, Tomás. Have you been having headaches?"

"I'm in the system. My whole life is a headache."

Santi held his tongue and waited the boy out.

He was rewarded with a rough exhalation. "Fine. Yes, sometimes my head hurts."

Elena wheeled herself a couple of inches closer. "Did the headaches start at the same time that your legs get worse?"

Tomás's mouth twisted. "I think so. So what does that mean?"

Not saying anything, Santi finished his

examination. "I'm not sure yet. But your lungs sound good and so does your belly. What I'm going to do next is send you for a CT scan. Do you know what that is?"

"Yes. I have a bad heart, remember? Lots of scans and tests."

"I'm sure you've had more than your share. But this time I want to look inside your head." He glanced at Elena, and she gave a slight nod as if to say she was thinking along the same lines.

He hoped they were both wrong. That there was nothing growing inside this kid's head. Although manipulating his neck hadn't brought forth anything, leaning forward to grasp Santi's hands sure had. And it was a similar movement to stretching across a table and to bending down to get his shoes. If there was a brain tumor growing in there, the changes in blood pressure by bending or hard stretching could theoretically cause pain, depending on where in the brain a growth was.

It was something to rule out. And better to start with the most grave possibility and work their way backward.

He pulled his cell phone out and put in the order.

"How long do I have to stay in there this time? Because I'll need to get my earbuds or something."

"I'll make sure you get some. And I don't know what tests you've had, but it might take longer. We may need to give you a little shot of dye if we can't see anything without it. You're not claustrophobic, are you?"

"It's going to happen even if I am, right?"

"Yes. It needs to. But I can give you something for anxiety if you need it."

"I don't need anything."

Yes, he did. Tomás just wasn't willing to admit it. Yet. But Santi hoped with time that they could build his trust. He'd talked about Caitlin leaving him just like everyone else, so it meant that he'd trusted the cardiologist. Most of this had to be rooted in fear. And honestly, Santi couldn't blame him. For any of it.

"Okay, then. They should be here in a few minutes to take you down. We'll be close by, though."

"You're going to watch?"

"We are. I want to make sure everything goes smoothly."

Was Tomás afraid of being alone? Of being left?

Hell, if anyone could relate to that, Santi could. Carmen's death had ticked both of those boxes. But if he could do anything here and now, he was going to make sure this boy didn't feel abandoned, like he'd obviously felt in the past.

He knew he should ask Elena, though, before including her in his plans. "Is that okay with you?"

"Yes." Her eyes met his and she gave a slight smile. "I don't know where anything is yet, so you'll need to direct me how to get there."

"You can follow me. Imaging is on the next floor up."

Elena backed her chair a few inches. "We'll see you soon, Tomás."

He answered with yet another shrug, but Santi could swear there was a hint of relief in the way his shoulders relaxed, in the way the tension in his jaw eased.

Just then a nurse came in and began to get things ready for the teen to be wheeled down.

That was their cue to leave. Santi could only hope the CT gave them the answers they wanted.

Elena pushed a button near the door, and it opened with a whisper of sound. She went through it. Turning slightly to look over her shoulder, she said, "You'll have to remind me where the elevators are."

He went ahead of her, walking with his normal speed in the direction they'd come earlier. "Let me know if I'm going too fast."

"You're not." There was a hint of irony to her words that wasn't lost on him.

He decided this was someone who didn't want or need him to ask about every little thing. If she needed him to change pace, she would tell him. He liked that. She'd been pretty direct at the wedding, too. It was one of the things that he'd found so attractive about her. Maybe that's why he'd ended up kissing her, when it was the last thing he should have done.

But man had it been good. That made it even worse.

They got to the elevator, and he pushed the up button. The car pinged as it arrived, the doors sliding apart. He put his arm across the mechanism, holding it open while she made her way inside. He got in, and she pushed the button for the next floor. They were the only passengers, and standing beside her, the ventilation system stirred the air, and he caught a slight whiff of clean lemon. From her shampoo? It tempted him to lean down and investigate a little more. If he pulled the tie from her hair, would those locks tumble down around her shoulders like they had that night, releasing more of that fragrance?

He gave an inward groan. *Stop it. Not the time. Or the place.*

Not that there was a right time or place. She was off-limits. Not just because of Carmen, but because of work as well. But why was that, really? What was it about business and pleasure that didn't mix?

Because things could get very messy very fast. And because he didn't do relationships or forever. Not anymore. Besides, he no longer believed that forever existed outside of romantic fiction. Or gorgeous wedding settings.

That had to be what it was. Why he'd been drawn to her. Why he was still drawn to her.

The elevator arrived at its destination before he had a chance to dissect that last statement. And just as well.

The imaging department was busy, as usual, and Tomás was sitting on his gurney, shoulders slumped, waiting his turn. The teen didn't look any happier now than he had in that room. While Elena went over to let him know they were there, Santi went to the desk to find out where they were in the queue.

The nurse checked her paperwork. "It shouldn't be long. He goes in as soon as the current patient comes out."

"Thanks."

He joined Elena and Tomás. "Looks like it will be just a few more minutes."

Tomás didn't look up, just continued staring at the floor. "It doesn't matter how long it is."

Santi gave an audible sigh that there was no change in the boy's attitude. He was surprised there wasn't a representative from the group home here as an advocate, but it could be they had more than one child here or had asked to be called if there was a problem. But despite the attitude, a pang went through him that the kid was having to handle this completely on his own. If Santi had had trouble handling things after Carmen's death, how much harder would it be for a kid like this?

"So what do you want to do when you get older?"

Tomás shrugged and for a second he didn't think the teen was going to answer. But finally he said, "I want to have a dog."

The ache in his chest grew. Most kids grew up dreaming of buying a home and having nice things. Tomás wanted a dog. A companion. Something that would never leave him or hand him back when the going got tough.

Maybe this is where he could make a connection.

Santi smiled. "I have a dog. She's a Labrador retriever named Sasha. I could bring her in to meet you, if you'd like."

A pair of dark brown eyes swung up. "Hospitals don't let dogs come inside."

Okay, so it wasn't actually a yes. But it wasn't a no.

Sasha had been his and Carmen's. He'd brought her home as a puppy from a nearby shelter while his wife had been going through treatment. Carmen had loved that dog, whom she never got to see grow up into an adult. Sasha was now going on seven. And with every year that went by, he was aware that one of his last links to his wife would be severed when Sasha died.

Although she wasn't a certified therapy dog, Santi had taken Sasha through training so that she could be brought in to see Carmen. It had worked like a charm. It had also sparked his interest in hippotherapy— where horses were paired with differently abled people as a form of therapy. His background with the polo ponies on his dad's ranch in Argentina helped him realize how important the partnership between an equine and a person could be.

"They'll let Sasha in. She has special training. How about tomorrow? She can spend the day with me in my office. I have a couch in there. Maybe we could even arrange for you to hang out in there as well, rather than in your hospital room, to keep Sasha company." He eyed the teen. "As long as you don't overdo it."

"I don't have anywhere else to be. So I might as well be there."

Had he just seen a crack in Tomás's demeanor? Time would tell.

"I think Sasha would appreciate that. Thank you." He understood the need not to appear weak. Especially in a boy of his age who'd bounced from place to place. He didn't want to form attachments.

Santi could relate to that all too well.

He glanced at Elena and found that she was staring at him. What? She didn't like dogs?

She turned and wheeled away without a word, making him frown.

"Tomás, would you excuse me for a minute?"

He went over to where she was. "You disapprove of me bringing Sasha to visit him?"

When she glanced up at him, her eyes were bright. A little too bright.

"On the contrary. I approve. I really approve. I just…" She shook her head as if she couldn't find the right words. "I think that is just what Tomás needs right now. He's scared out of his wits, despite his bravado."

"I know. And we need him to cooperate if

we're going to help him. Maybe Sasha can provide him with some company, if nothing else. I'll check and make sure that's okay with the people responsible for him, and that the nurses know where to find him. Since my office is on the same floor as his hospital room, I don't think it'll be a problem."

She smiled. "You'd better be careful, or you'll have everyone in the pediatric wing clamoring for their turn with you and Sasha."

Including her?

There was something about her smile that punched him right in the chest. That made him want to take a step or two closer to catch another hint of that elusive fragrance he'd noticed on the elevator. He forced himself to stay where he was.

"Sasha has come to the hospital several times with me, especially if I know I'm going to be working late and don't want to ask my housekeeper to stay over."

"And the hospital is okay with that?"

"She's well behaved. And the kids seem to love her. Especially in her Christmas elf costume."

"Your dog has costumes."

There was shock and an element of bland

amusement in her voice that he liked. As if his words had been truly unexpected. "Several, actually."

She blinked. "You're very…surprising, you know that?"

"Am I?" He let one side of his mouth slide up in a half smile, not wanting her to see how much her words warmed him.

No one spoke for several seconds.

Elena glanced back. "Well, I think they're ready for him. Can you tell me where the observation room is?"

"Yep, I'll take you there."

Elena had needed to get away. Something about the idea of a strong man like Santi putting a costume on his dog and bringing her in to mingle with his young patients had made her heart clench. And his offer to let Tomás stay in his office with the dog had brought tears to her eyes. She needed to be careful. There was something about him that made her want to trust him. To move closer to him like she had at Caitlin's wedding. But she'd been burned going down that road once before.

Her professor had shown an interest in

her while she was in his class, and like any student, she'd developed a crush on him. He never asked her out while she was at the school, but a few weeks after she graduated, Renato called her and asked her to dinner. She'd been thrilled. His noticing hadn't just been part of her imagination. He actually had liked her. And she had liked him. A lot. Enough to be a nervous wreck as she'd spoken to him on the phone.

Dinner had been at a swanky, intimate restaurant. The atmosphere as they ate had quickly changed, little touches over the table leading to her going back to his apartment with him. And when he'd kissed her, the sparks had ignited.

Just like they had with Santi.

Renato had carried her to bed and had been an attentive lover, taking a lot of time with her. But then at the height of passion, he'd rolled onto his back and tried to haul her on top of him to straddle his hips. "Sit on me, *querida*."

Horror had zipped through her.

"I—I can't," she'd stammered, the blood rushing from her head. How could he not know that?

He'd sat up dragging a hand through his hair and apologizing profusely, but the mood had been completely shattered. While her paralysis wasn't complete and she could bear weight on her left leg—bracing herself with her arms—long enough to transfer from one place to the other, it didn't mean that she could do everything other people could. It hadn't been his fault. Not really.

But it had evidently bothered him enough that he'd never contacted her again. She'd been devastated. But even if he'd called, she didn't think she would have gone out with him again. And she wasn't sure why.

It had left her wary of being caught in a situation like that again. After Renato, she'd never let a date go further than dinner and a chaste kiss, not that there'd been many over the years. She was pretty sure she now gave off warning vibes that could be read for miles.

But Santi… Well, the man was a temptation. A big one. They worked together, though, which would amplify any awkwardness if she got carried away and then suddenly found she…couldn't.

And aside from that one kiss in the library, he'd shown no signs of wanting to kiss her again. For that she was grateful. It made things so much easier.

The observation room was surprisingly large with several open areas near the chairs where she could park with ease. She had a feeling Letizia had a hand in designing this room. She could move freely and change locations depending on what angle she wanted to see. Letizia said Aelina was the model she wanted other hospitals in Spain to use when they were thinking about accessibility.

And she was also surprised that there even *was* such a large observation room in the imaging department. Those were normally reserved for surgical areas of the hospital, although the booth where the techs sat usually had a couple of extra chairs where doctors could watch the scans roll out.

She'd expected Santi to go in there, actually. But he made no move to leave.

"They're getting ready to put him through." Santi settled in a chair next to her. "The tech will let us know if they see anything. And I'll decide then about the need for a dye."

The glass wasn't one-way and when Tomás glanced at the window, Santi gave him a thumbs-up sign to let him know they were there. Not that the boy returned it or even acknowledged the sign.

"Are you thinking tumor?" She hoped he wouldn't concentrate all his efforts on this one possibility. She preferred to keep things wide open and narrow them down a little at a time.

"No, it's just a starting place. Ruling this out lets us move on to the next possibility. Any thoughts?"

"I have several. A dystrophy, MS—"

"MS? I know it's possible, but I haven't come across a case of multiple sclerosis in a child yet."

"It's rare, but I don't want to rule anything out. Like I said, some of the dystrophies. Spinal cord lesions. The laundry list of possibilities is pretty long." She paused. "Caitlin said they looked at everything they could think of that was related to his heart, but there's still the possibility of neuropathy caused by perfusion issues."

Neuropathy could strike any part of the body that involved nerves. Elena experienced it herself with her injury. Although the attacks weren't as bad as they were after her fall, there were still times when she got zings of pain near what she called her dead zone. The band that separated the numb areas of her body and the areas where she retained feeling. Most especially in her left hip and thigh. Hers wasn't caused by perfusion problems, however, but by her spinal cord injury.

"Perfusion certainly makes it a little harder to identify the cause, since his circulatory system isn't ideal. But from the looks of it, Tomás has done better than some of the other hypoplastic left heart syndrome patients. The survival rates are better than they used to be, but chronic lack of oxygen eventually takes its toll."

"Yes, it does. Caitlin said he could go on the transplant list if and when that started to become an issue."

The flat bed area of the CT machine started to move into the doughnut-shaped hole, stopping when Tomás's head was inside the field. The tech's voice came through. "Try to hold your head and neck very still, Tomás, okay?"

No response.

Although the teen appeared to be doing as he was told, she could tell by the flexing and unflexing of his feet that the position wasn't comfortable for him.

"Santi…"

"I see him." The pediatrician paused. "He said sitting was the most comfortable for him. I've been trying to puzzle through why that is. Although he said when he was sitting on the bed and reaching down for his shoes he had an attack of pain. Which is why it made me think the problem was positional."

Santi pulled out his tablet and scrolled through whatever was on the screen. He glanced over at her. "They did a tilt table test on him and there were no major changes in his blood pressure."

"I'm going to try to sit down with his chart tonight and comb through everything and see if I can find any holes in his testing. Although Caitlin is very thorough."

"Maybe we can brainstorm that together in my office tomorrow. Sasha will be there to keep Tomás company, and he'll be close by in case either of us have any questions for him. Hopefully he'll start opening up more."

That made sense. There were times, though, when she liked to really sit down by herself and study the charts. But she could do that tonight. At least she thought she could. "Can I access patient files remotely? I'm staying in one of the staff housing units across the park and would like to get up to speed on everything."

"Yep, just ask HR for the code, if you're doing it from a different device than the one in your office."

"Okay, thanks. I'll check in with them." Before she could capture her next words, she blurted out, "Are you staying in the housing area as well?"

He glanced at her. "No. I live about twenty minutes from here."

The words were a little curt, and she couldn't blame him. It was really none of her business where he lived.

Cielos! Did he think she was making a pass at him? She wasn't. And she wasn't even sure why she'd asked the question. It was just straight-up curiosity. One that she needed to toss aside before it got her into trouble.

Like with that kiss?

Yes. Exactly like that. Except she hadn't really tossed it completely aside, because she kept thinking about it.

If she were smart, she would weigh any future words with care. The last thing she needed was to make Santi uncomfortable or give him the wrong idea.

The same went for her. She had to make sure she got no funny ideas about the handsome pediatrician, not if she wanted to continue to enjoy her time at Santa Aelina.

CHAPTER FOUR

THE PARK WAS nicer than she expected. Her racing chair flew down the pathway, and she passed a jogger who was traveling at a nice leisurely pace. Elena did leisurely during her nights working at the hospital. The evening shifts were like that. Quiet with periods of frenetic activity.

When she got off work at six in the morning, she wanted a real workout. Felt the need for speed. Maybe it mimicked what she used to have when she raced Strato across the beach on days they weren't training for competitions. She sighed. Those days were over, although Sandra had offered to help her get on Strato, if she wanted to try to ride again. She did. But she'd been too angry at her condition over those first six months to even think about it. And she'd been afraid she wouldn't be able to mount, much less handle any kind of cues involving her legs.

Then she went to college and her days had grown busy.

And now?

She wasn't sure what held her back. Maybe the idea that she could never have what she'd had before. She wasn't sure she could stand the sting of regret or the what-ifs that might follow.

She turned another sharper corner in the running path, the cool morning invigorating her and loosening her muscles. Suddenly she had to swerve hard to avoid another jogger coming at her from the opposite direction. "Sorry!" She threw the word over her shoulder before realizing the person had stopped and turned in her direction and was now jogging after her. Worse, she now recognized who it was.

Dios! It was Santi. What the hell was he doing out here? She thought he'd said he didn't live in the hospital housing unit.

That didn't mean he couldn't use the park. It was for anyone, whether they lived on-site or not.

The impulse to put on a burst of speed and

try to outpace him came and went. What would doing that accomplish besides make it obvious she didn't want to interact with him? And it would make working with him even more awkward.

She wasn't embarrassed that he'd found her getting some exercise. No, her avoidance radar had to do more with that stupid kiss than her physical condition.

Every time she saw him, she still pictured the exact moment when he leaned closer… when she realized what was about to happen. The second her eyelids slid closed in dreamy bliss. And the first glorious touch had been—

"You're out and about early." The gravel of his voice stopped her wayward thoughts, and her fingers tightened around the wheels of her chair, arms almost forgetting to keep pumping. She forced herself to concentrate. The last thing she wanted to do was jerk to a stop and dump herself onto the ground.

It's not that she couldn't brace her left knee on the ground and use her arms to haul herself back into the chair. She could. But even before her accident, she would have been embarrassed to fall flat on her face in front of someone.

And she still worked her legs, putting a brace on the one that still had a modicum of feeling left and using it to support her weight. But she did that in a more controlled setting, which reminded her that she needed to find a gym with a trainer who specialized in spinal cord injuries. Working her muscles in the pool was her favorite way to train. That and propelling herself in her racing chair.

"Early? Well, I just got off work and ran home to change clothes and chairs. I could ask you the same question." Why did she sound so much breathier than he did?

"Could you slow down for a minute?"

The surprising request made her muscles go slack instantly, and only then did she realize her arms were shaking. Not so much from exertion but from nerves.

He slowed to a walk, glancing at her. "I do like your ride, by the way. Especially the reflective fabric."

Her racing chair was neon orange with those reflective flecks woven right in to help make her more visible. Sometimes runners whose line of sight was over her head and who were "in the zone" might not notice her until she had to jerk sideways to avoid them. This way, their peripheral vision caught sight of something other than green trees or asphalt.

"The better to see you with, my dear." The lines of the well-known fairy tale came out before she could stop them.

"Or maybe to be seen?"

She blinked, surprised he'd caught her drift so easily, without her having to explain. She nodded. "I'm easy to miss."

His mouth twisted slightly. "Oh, I know for a fact that's not true."

A shiver went through her. He wasn't talking about the same thing she was. And her tongue tripped over several flippant responses before the truth came out. "You'd be surprised how invisible you feel, sometimes." Going from almost five foot ten at eighteen to about half that height sitting down had been one of the biggest shocks she'd had to get used to. She'd always been visible. Sometimes painfully so. How silly it seemed now to be so embarrassed about being tall.

In an instant her life had changed in almost every way. From the way she ambulated, to the way she drove a vehicle…to the way she made love. She could still do it all. The mechanics just had to be tweaked.

She glanced down at her breeches. They were one of the last remnants of her riding days, but one that she held on to. She found that the grippiness the garment had afforded her in an English saddle worked to keep her stuck in her chair when she was racing across a surface or while shifting her weight to navigate tight turns. The same things she'd done while riding.

But those knee patches might look weird to Santi. If so, he didn't say anything.

Instead, he smiled. "Someday I'll race you."

He hadn't offered platitudes or tried to convince her that how she felt wasn't real or valid. A weird pinging sensation started in the region of her heart, and she had to force herself not to visibly react. She understood that people wanted to make her feel better, but they didn't realize that sometimes it just made her feel worse. Like no one understood. But Santi hadn't done that. In fact, he acted like he really did understand what she went through sometimes. How?

"You mean as in chair against chair?"

"I think you might have an unfair advantage there."

She laughed. No one had ever even hinted at that before. She decided to go with it. "I think I might have an unfair advantage whether you're on foot or on wheels."

His smile widened, showing a flash of white teeth. "Is that a challenge, Dr. Solis?"

Was it? Exactly how dangerous would it be to challenge a man like Santi? Probably very dangerous. But since when had she shied away from things that weren't so safe?

"It is indeed, Dr. Garcia."

"Be careful what you wish for. It might just come true."

Elena pushed a lock of hair out of her eyes, trying to ferret out the expression on his face. But it suddenly shuttered against her probing stare, his smile disappearing in an instant. The same way Renato's face and demeanor had changed during their love-making session.

Her chest tightened. She and Santi had never been involved. Had certainly never made love. Barely even knew each other. So why did she feel a boulder in the place where her stomach normally sat?

His cell phone pinged, and he pulled it out of one of the pockets of his navy jogging pants, glancing at the screen just as her phone went off, too. Another sense of foreboding settled over her.

She pulled her phone out of her belt bag and looked at it. It was from Grace Rivas, a midwife she'd consulted with briefly in the past and met in person on her first day at Aelina.

Emergency situation. Can you come back to Aelina?

Caitlin had told her how Grace and her husband, Diego, had patched up their rocky marriage.

She and Santi looked up from their devices at the same time. Their eyes met.

"I need to go."

Their words matched syllable for syllable, and his face softened. "They called you back, too?"

"Yes. Any idea what it is?"

"No, just that it's a teen and the other pediatrician is stuck in traffic." He nodded at her chair. "Are you okay to work in that?"

"Yep. Let's go."

They raced back to the hospital and when they got to the desk, Carlos, one of the ER nurses, stopped them. "They're up in maternity."

Santi frowned. "Are you sure that's the right patient?"

"Yes. Very."

"Thanks, we'll head up."

That was weird. Pediatrics was on the third floor while maternity was on the first. She could understand being called to a case there, but Santi? He wasn't a neonatologist.

They went up the elevator, with Elena trying not to be weirded out at going to work in breeches, of all things. At least the sweat had dried in the air-conditioning. She'd been dragging when she'd left the building, but her workout and the adrenaline of knowing there was an emergency had reenergized her.

And maybe that had a little to do with meeting Santi on the path?

Diablos, she hoped not.

The doors opened and Grace met them.

"Thanks for getting here so fast. I'm about to have the patient wheeled down to the maternal intensive care area. She's now comatose."

As they went back to the room, Grace filled them in. "Sixteen-year-old who's twenty-four weeks pregnant. She's been emancipated and is technically married, but neither her parents nor the baby's father are in the picture anymore. A friend called paramedics when they found her passed out on the floor." She paused to take a breath as they reached the doorway. "We've taken bloods, but her sugar is normal, which is the first thing both Diego and I thought of—he's prepping for a different surgery, which is part of the reason I needed you guys back. It's a race to figure out what is going on."

That was why Santi was here. At sixteen, the patient was still considered a pediatric case in some areas despite the emancipation.

Elena's mind went through a labyrinth of possible causes. Gestational diabetes would have been high on her list as well. But with no elevated sugar...

"And the baby?" Santi had gloved up and was now standing over the patient already doing his own examination and Elena moved to the area beside him.

"A quick ultrasound reveals everything as it should be. No molar pregnancy. Nothing to suggest that the pregnancy itself is to blame. But the baby's vitals are showing some downward trends that we need to correct, if we hope to save either of them."

Molar pregnancies—when the beginnings of a fetus turn into a tumor that overtake everything and threaten the life of the mother—could be fatal in and of themselves. But this was a viable pregnancy.

She began to sort through some options. "Tell me if something I throw out isn't something you've looked at. Stroke—" she paused as she went through the list being generated in her head and watched Grace for a reaction to each "—brain tumor, cancer of any type—"

"We haven't gotten as far as MRIs and such. She's just come in. We've only had time to check the baby and her. She really needs to be down the hall in ICU. But I didn't want to move her until you saw her."

"Blood ox is low. COVID?"

"We did two rapid tests for that and the flu. Both came back negative."

Elena's head tilted as something caught her eye. "Santi, look at her neck."

His gaze shifted as he looked. "What am I… Wait. I think I see something." He palpated her throat and then fingered a strand of hair. "Hmm… Did you send for thyroid levels?"

"I did. I asked them to be expedited."

"Okay. Heart rate is low. So are respirations."

Elena pulled down the sheet and checked the girl's ankles. "Puffy here and so are her hands."

"I noticed that, too," Grace said. "Which is why I thought maybe diabetes. You're thinking she has hypothyroidism? That makes sense. She's not had prenatal exams from what I'm gathering. Unfortunately, I'm seeing more and more of this in younger patients who are trying to hide pregnancies. I had a case like that just a few weeks ago that was touch and go."

Grace's phone rang. "This may be it." She put the device to her ear. "Mmm-hmm…

Oh, wow. I think that explains it. Thanks. Send over the numbers, okay?"

She hung up. "You were right. Extremely high THS. They're sending over the labs."

Elena breathed a sigh of relief. "What we know, we can treat."

"Absolutely," Santi agreed. "Checking dosages now. Let's go ahead and move her and add some levothyroxine to her drip. I also want to start hydrocortisone in case there's pituitary involvement besides just her low thyroid levels." He looked at her as if seeking her opinion.

"I agree. If we're right, we should start seeing some improvement pretty quickly. I want her to stay on oxygen until her blood ox is above ninety percent."

Grace reached down and gave her hand a squeeze. "Thank you. To both of you."

"You're more than welcome." Elena smiled back. "I want to know how she and the baby do."

Santi got off the phone call he'd made as she and Grace had been talking. "I've called Dario Mileno, who's still a few minutes away. He agrees with treatment and will come down to see her when he arrives. He's seen one of these before. This is my first."

"Who's Dario Mileno?" Elena hadn't yet met everyone on staff. Working more on the night shift made it hard.

"He's our endocrinologist. He's one of the best. She'll be in good hands." Santi glanced at her. "Are you exhausted, or can you hang around for a few minutes in case Grace needs us back?"

Grace nodded. "I would really appreciate that. And good catch, you two."

"Elle did the catching. If she hadn't noticed her neck, we might still be looking."

The midwife's eyes widened, mimicking her own, which Elena tried to hide. Normally only her good friends called her that. The fact that Santi had…

Meant nothing. She'd called him by a shortened version of his name lots of times, so why was it different for him to do the same? It wasn't. But her heart had given a hard couple of thumps when he had. And that mellow voice curling around that one syllable…? Oh, man. It might turn her to goo, and that was not good.

She covered her reaction the best she

could. "The TSH numbers would have cued you in. We all did our part."

"So we did." Santi moved so the two nurses who came in could gather equipment and move the bed to a room down the hall where at-risk pregnancy patients could be monitored. "Are you good, Grace?"

"I think we have it under control now. I'll text you in a few minutes once we get the drip started."

Another man crowded into the room, and he and Santi shook hands. "I just got in. Have you started treatment yet?"

"They're just moving her now," Santi said. He then turned to Elena. "Dario, this is Elena Solis. She's our new diagnostician."

His head tilted as he looked at her. "Didn't I work with you once? Over at Santa Pedro's a year or so ago?"

"Oh, yes, I do remember. The dengue case that came in from Brazil."

"That's the one."

For some reason it felt good to have Santi see that she actually did know what she was doing. Most of the time, anyway. It seemed her brain worked in a way that other people didn't always understand. But that was probably due to her trying to absorb every minute detail about the way her body had worked before and after the accident. It was almost as if she could float above the scene and "see" it. Could put things together that didn't always seem to go together.

Dario smiled at her. "Okay if I consult with you from time to time when you're around?"

"I will be around. I've decided to settle in at Aelina's for a while."

"Great! No more roaming from place to place?"

Her eyes darted to Santi and saw him frown. What was wrong? Was he sorry she was staying at Aelina's? He hadn't seemed that way a minute or so ago, but now...?

Her chin lifted as if daring the pediatrician to say something. "No, not for the foreseeable future."

"Very good. I'll see if I can drum you up some work." Dario gave her another smile, moving so they could wheel the patient out of the room. "But for now, I have patients to see. Check in with me when you get a chance. I'm on the fifth floor."

Her eyes widened. "That's where I'll be once I'm done in pediatrics."

"Well how lucky is that? Looks like we'll be seeing a lot of each other."

The endocrinologist followed the patient from the room.

Once he had disappeared from sight, Grace bumped shoulders with her and gave her a smile. She didn't say anything, but she knew what the other woman was thinking. And she agreed. Dario Mileno had been flirting with her. If Grace could see it then maybe… When she looked again at Santi, she saw that she was right. He'd noticed. And he didn't look happy about it.

Why? It wasn't like *he'd* shown a lot of interest in her. Oh, he'd been friendly, but the way he'd recoiled from that kiss had stung.

Still stung, if she were honest with herself, and to have a man show some interest in her helped soothe that hurt just a bit.

She started to say goodbye to Grace and the other woman said, "When you have some time, I can show you around the area, if you want. You're staying in the housing on the other side of the park, right?"

"I am. And I would love for you to show

me what's what. I'm the last house on the left when you step off the pathway. Come over sometime."

"Thanks. I will." She threw Santi a smile. "Stop looking so grumpy. You haven't looked so put out since Carm…" Her words died away, and she looked mortified. "That didn't come out right. I'm sorry."

"It's okay. And I'm not grumpy. It's just a been a long night. To prove it, I'll treat you both to breakfast. Cafeteria style."

Grace wrinkled her nose. "No thanks. Besides, I have babies to deliver. Take Elena. She needs to experience El Café Aelina at least once." With that, the midwife walked out the door.

She was quick to try to retract the other woman's offer. "You don't have to—"

"Yes, I do. Besides, Grace is right. You do need to experience it. At least once."

He escorted her out of the room and down the hallway, making Elena wonder what the hell to think. One minute there were storm clouds hanging over his head and the next…?

Well, she had no idea what was hanging over his head now. Except for trouble. Trouble that Elena would do well to avoid.

CHAPTER FIVE

ME CAE GORDO. Maybe Santi was being irrational, but Dario Mileno really did rub him the wrong way. Ever since they'd almost come to blows that day when Carmen was having tests run at the hospital. Before she was diagnosed.

Thinking about that would do no good. And Carmen had insisted the man wasn't flirting with her. But Santi remembered exactly how he'd felt when he laid eyes on her for the first time. He'd been completely *enamorado.* If there ever was a love at first sight, it had been that day she'd come to visit Argentina and had wound up on one of his father's polo ponies. Santi had been on another, actively hitting the ball around with some colleagues, when she trotted over and asked to join the game.

Her accent, the way she moved with this unconscious seductive air, had bowled him over and he'd been...*enamorado*. There was no other word for it. They'd exchanged numbers and when she flew back to Spain ten days later he'd called her. He was already a doctor at the time. And soon he was applying at hospitals in Spain. He'd jumped at the first position in Barcelona. The rest was history.

And now it really was history.

As he walked beside Elle, he tried not to think about how Dario had brought all those memories back with his talk of collaborating with the new diagnostician. Maybe Carmen had been right. Maybe it was all in his imagination. But he didn't think so. The endocrinologist had dated a lot of female staff on the fifth floor, and it never seemed to end well.

A little girl stood in a doorway as they neared the end of the hallway and stared at Elle.

"Are you going home? Where's your baby?"

A voice called from inside the room. "Maria! Don't ask such questions!

But Elena didn't flinch. "It's okay. She's fine."

Her voice was soft as she continued. "I'm not going home. Not yet. And I don't have a baby."

The child's tiny brow puckered. "But my mom said she has to be wheeled out like that."

Santi's chest tightened. His mouth opened to stop the questioning when a hand touched his.

Elena glanced up at him. "I like answering questions." She turned back to Maria. "I'm not riding in this chair because I'm going home. I'm in it because I have to be. I can't walk, like you can."

Her words were so even. So full of confidence that it took him aback. It had never crossed his mind to ask her what happened. Maybe because of his work with hippotherapy.

"Why? You have legs."

That made Elena laugh. "I do, don't I? But mine don't work the way yours do. You see I was riding a beautiful black horse a long time ago. It was like I was riding the wind. I loved my horse very much. And then I fell." She smiled at the child. "Have you ever fallen down?"

The girl gave her a grave nod. "I hurt my knee when I fell once. I cried."

"Well, I got hurt like that. And I hurt my knee, too. But I also hurt my back, very badly. So badly that my legs can't hold me up anymore. So I ride in this chair."

"It looks like fun."

"It is. Sometimes."

Maria seemed to ponder that for a minute. "Do you have a picture of your horse?"

"I do, but I don't have it with me. His full name is Vientos de la Estratosfera, but I call him Strato for short."

"That's a funny name."

Santi kind of liked it. Winds of the Stratosphere. He could picture just the kind of horse he was. And Elle probably did feel like the wind when she rode him.

Her riding trousers suddenly made sense, and his chest tightened even farther. Were these like the breeches she'd worn when she'd been hurt? She'd mentioned that she rode when they were at the wedding, when they'd seen that crazy picture in the library. But he'd had no idea she'd injured her back while doing so.

"It is a funny name. But he's a funny horse."

Said as if the horse was still alive. And maybe he was. Maybe Elena kept tabs on him. He could see her doing that.

"Maria, that's enough, come back inside and help me with your baby brother."

"Okay." She turned back to Elena. "I have to go. I hope you have fun with your horse."

Elena smiled, but her lips had tightened. She waved at the child and started moving away from the door.

"I'm sorry, I didn't know."

She shrugged. "Well, now you do."

They didn't say anything further until they got to the ground floor, where the cafeteria was. They entered the eatery and Elena expertly went through the line making choices and asking for help when she couldn't reach something. Santi remembered the first time he was at the café line at the first hospital he'd worked at. Everything had looked so different from what he was used to in Argentina, but he'd liked it. And later, he'd learned he wasn't supposed to like hospital food. At least everyone else complained about it. Even Grace had.

They sat down at a table just as Elle got a text from someone. She looked at it. "Dario says treatment has started, and he'll let us know when there's some improvement. He says he's hopeful. About a lot of..." Her voice died away, and he could swear he saw a hint of color flush her cheeks.

Dammit. He was right. Even Elle... Elena knew. When had he started thinking of her as Elle? He wasn't sure.

"He's hopeful about a lot of things, huh? I think maybe Grace's sly hints are right."

"Of course they're not. I'm sure he was just talking about the patient's chances of recovery."

Whatever she said. But he didn't believe it. And he didn't think she did, either.

"Well, I'm glad he thinks his chances are good." Too late he realized he'd made a Freudian slip and made it sound like Dario thought *his* chances were good rather than their patient—who was a girl.

She giggled, killing his hopes that she'd misunderstood his words. "I'm pretty sure *he* has no chance at all."

"I'm not telling you anything that's not

common knowledge when I say that Dario Mileno has a bit of a reputation."

"I know. I can spot them a mile away. Now."

Said as if there was a time when she couldn't. "Sorry. I had no right to say anything."

"No, I appreciate it. It's just that I can take care of myself."

"Of that I have no doubt." He was seeing more and more of that in her. She was a self-assured, confident woman. Maybe that's what had struck him about her. Carmen had been the same, but underneath there'd been this kind of vulnerability about her that brought out his protective instincts. That was probably what had led him to warn her about Dario. What Carmen hadn't been able to see—because she always saw the best in everybody—Elle had spotted in an instant. Because of what had happened to her? Because she relied on herself? Probably.

But more than that, she'd made it sound like she'd met Dario's type before. Maybe had even been pulled in by someone.

Demonio! He hoped not.

She popped a grape into her mouth, while

he struggled for something to say. "So I knew you rode before, from what you said the first time we met. But I didn't realize you'd had a horse of your own. Where did you grow up?"

"In Mallorca, actually. I was a typical horse-crazy girl. My parents brought home a pony." She smiled. "I was ecstatic. Except Bom-Bom didn't match his name. He wasn't a good-good boy. He was actually quite *travieso* and liked to stand on my foot, or zig when I asked him to zag. Maybe my parents thought it would cure me. But it just made me more determined. Then, when I was a little older, they bought Strato. And that was it. He was…*is*…my heart horse. Always will be."

She had certainly made it sound like he was when she was describing the horse to Maria a few minutes ago.

"I had a favorite horse as well."

"Tell me about him." She leaned her chin on her palm and looked at him across the table.

"His name was Diablo."

"Wow. Did he live up to his name?"

One side of his mouth quirked. "He did

in more ways than one. He could be a devil. But he was also a devil to catch, which came in handy on the polo field. I think my family was disappointed in my decision to become a doctor rather than helping run the business."

"I can imagine."

He shifted the subject back to her to avoid going into some of the heated discussions that had transpired when he told his dad what he wanted out of life. "Do you still ride?"

"No. A good friend is taking care of Strato. He deserves the best life can offer. I'll probably never ride again."

That surprised him. "Why?"

She looked at him as if in disbelief. "Strato wouldn't know what to do with me."

"He could be retrained. There are lots of ways."

"And sometimes there aren't." Her mouth tightened. "Do *you* still ride?"

"Yes. Not as often as I'd like, and it's been a while."

"Oh." She deflated as if she'd been expecting to question him on his decision, like he'd questioned hers.

"I actually met my wife while riding. Carmen loved horses. She introduced me to hippotherapy."

Was he still trying to steer her toward the idea that riding wasn't beyond her grasp?

"You're married?"

Oh, hell, she'd latched onto the wrong thing. And her question was anything but curious. There was an anger behind the words that he totally understood and was quick to correct.

"Carmen died six years ago."

Her cheeks burned with color like they'd done when Dario had texted her a few minutes ago. "I'm so sorry. I just thought…"

"You were angry that I would kiss you, if I was married. Believe me. I wouldn't have. I never cheated on her. It never even crossed my mind."

"I should have realized. I'm sorry again."

"It's okay. Unlike Dario, I have no reputation. None at all."

That got a smile out of her. "None? Surely everyone is known for something."

"Hmm. Then what about you? What are you known for?" He wanted to know what she thought people saw when they looked at her.

"I think I'm known for solving puzzles."

Ah, that made sense, especially with the work she did. It wasn't quite what he'd been looking for, but he wasn't going to backtrack and try to make her rephrase her answer. He'd asked...and she'd told him. *El fin*.

It also explained why he'd told her about Carmen, when he rarely talked about her, not even to the people at the hospital. Ones who had known her. Elena was good at coaxing information from patients. He'd seen that for himself with Tomás.

With a wry chuckle, he said, "And from the looks of it, you're very good at finding the pieces to whatever puzzle you might be trying to solve." Like trying to solve the puzzle of him? Not likely. Santi didn't know if there was anything left to solve.

"Thanks. I try. But I don't always succeed."

"I don't think any of us can claim to solve one hundred percent of the cases we're given. All we can do is try. And when it's not enough, when there's nothing left to be done... We have to accept that, too."

Like he'd done with his wife, when he'd wanted to try treatment after treatment, hoping for a magic bullet that would kill her cancer. She'd finally said enough and called hospice herself. By that time, the disease had overwhelmed her system, and he realized how stupid he'd been to throw away the time they could have spent building memories. It should have been Carmen's call all along.

When Elena started speaking again, he shook away the thoughts.

"So are you involved with hippotherapy?"

"I volunteer at a center called En Alas de Caballo."

She blinked, then slowly repeated the words. "'On horses' wings.' I like that. I always did feel like I was flying."

It was on the tip of his tongue to say she could still feel that way, but she'd made it pretty clear that riding wasn't something she saw herself doing. At least not right now. And he wasn't going to push where he wasn't welcome. But he could offer something else.

"I'd be happy to take you over to see it. I take a group of kids from the hospital over there once a month to see and interact with the horses. This Friday is the day, actually. There would be no strings attached. I'm not trying to convince you to ride or anything else. I've taken a lot of Aelina's staff over there. A few of them even volunteer."

She stared down at her plate for a moment or two before lifting her head to look at him. "I think I'd like that. No strings attached, though, right?"

"Not even a little one." A weight seemed to roll off him, and he wasn't sure why. Maybe because he was so passionate about the equine therapy center that he wanted to share that love with others. Or maybe he really did hope she'd eventually get back on a horse.

"How do you even find time to volunteer? From what I've seen, your night-shift work takes up most of your time."

It does, but Friday afternoons are sacrosanct. There are two other pediatricians who have offered to work a few hours in the evening so I can go, and they trade off. It gives me time to be at the center to lead Billy."

"Billy?"

"Billy was my horse here in Spain. I donated him to On Horses' Wings six years ago."

"Six years ago…" She seemed to mull something over, then she gave a visible swallow.

She'd figured it out. And maybe like Elle, he'd given up something he loved after losing something he'd loved even more. "He has a good home. A good purpose. And I see him every single week. Billy and Lirio, his rider."

"I like your horse's name. Sounds like a cowboy name."

"He's kind of a cowboy horse. More like the Criollos of Argentina. Rugged and famous for endurance. Billy's not sleek and elegant like the Andalusians you have here in Spain."

"You live in Spain too, remember? Or did you never fully leave Argentina?"

"I think part of my heart will always be in my homeland. But I've chosen to make my home here in Barcelona."

"Even if you can't own another Criollo?"

"There's always a way. I've learned that every time I step into the arena with Billy and Lirio."

She sighed when her phone pinged again. But this time when she looked at her screen she smiled. "The patient's respiration and heart rate are going up. They're hoping she'll wake up soon. Baby's stats are improving along with his or her mom's." Her gaze traveled a little farther, and she rolled her eyes.

Evidently the endocrinologist was still hinting at something. He ignored her look and concentrated on what the body of the text had said.

"That's good news."

"Yes, it is." She sighed and picked up her now-empty tray, setting it in her lap. "And with that, I think I need to head home so I can shower and go to bed. Before my shift starts back up again tonight. I really want to work on Tomás's case and see if he'll tell us any more. He was still kind of sullen again when I visited him today."

"Same here. Maybe we should try to do like we did a couple of days ago. Go in together and tag team him. Maybe this time we'll be harder to resist as a pair."

The second the words were out of his mouth, he wished he could retract them. Maybe the traits he detested so much in

Dario were being transferred to him. Wasn't that what they said happened? That if you weren't careful you'd take on your enemy's characteristics?

Demonio! If so, he'd better damn well put a stop to it. Before she started rolling her eyes at him, too.

Instead she smiled and said something completely unexpected. And completely unsettling.

"Yes. Maybe we are."

Grace called her the next afternoon, just as she'd pulled on her clothes for work. Her heart started pounding. "Our hypothyroid patient?"

"Yes. I just came in a few minutes ago, and Patricia is awake. Thought you might like to hear."

"That is great news, Grace, thanks for letting me know!"

"I hope you don't mind me calling your cell phone."

She smiled. "Of course not. I don't know very many people at the hospital, so it's nice to get a phone call relaying happy news. I don't always hear the results when I've worked on cases."

"Well, this time you will. Her THS numbers are coming down, too. They're thinking maybe something autoimmune crashed her thyroid. But for now it looks like the levothyroxine and cortisone combination are going to do the trick."

"When is she going to be discharged?"

"Probably tomorrow or the day after."

"Fantastic. I hope she starts coming in for follow-ups. She needs to be seen regularly, especially expecting at such a young age."

"Yes, and having no support system to boot. Hey, do you want to go out for dinner before work tomorrow? Diego has surgery scheduled earlier that day, so I'll be on my own and could use some company."

Elena pulled in a breath, a sense of relief washing through her. "I would love that, thank you."

She'd wondered if she would like being stuck in one hospital, if she would have enough work or feel like an outsider, but so far she really liked Aelina. Despite some of her uneasy feelings about Santi. Most of those were of her own making, though. It wasn't like he'd made her feel unwelcome. In fact, they seemed to work well together, most of the time, which in itself made her feel odd.

Maybe we're harder to resist as a pair.

She didn't know about them as a pair, but one thing she did know. He was pretty hard to resist all on his own. After their conversation this morning over breakfast, she'd been unable to resist looking up Criollos. They might not look like Strato—who was as Andalusian as they came—but they were beautiful in their own right. She'd expected something scruffier from Santi's description. Instead she'd found they came in different colors, many with at least some kind of roaning—where a darker-hair coat was interspersed with white. They were known for their agility and quite popular as polo ponies. Which made complete sense, given what he'd told her about his family's polo business.

She arrived at the hospital and decided to peek into Letizia's office. "Just wanted to say hi."

"Well, hi, yourself. I've been meaning

to sneak up to the third floor and see how you're doing. Aelina is treating you okay?"

She pulled the door farther open. "It is."

"And the case with Dr. Garcia?"

"We haven't found the answer quite yet, but we're still working on it. I'm heading up there in a few minutes."

"If I know you, you won't quit until you get to the bottom of it. That's what makes you so good at your job."

There were some things she might never get to the bottom of. Like the reason she'd gotten so defensive when Santi had asked her about riding. Because when he'd asked her to go to the equine therapy center, a trill of excitement had shot through her. Why? It wasn't like she was going to ride one of those horses. Maybe it was the thought of seeing a horse again.

Or maybe it was the hint of excitement over accompanying him somewhere outside the hospital.

Well, whatever it was, she'd better get a hold of that feeling and quick. Once she did, she needed to fling it so far away that she'd forget all about it. Ha! Like that was even a possibility.

Well, it needed to be not only a possibility, she also had to work to make it her reality. Before something happened that she might regret.

Something far worse than going to the center with him. Far worse than the simple kiss they'd shared. Something subtle kept hanging around trying to get her to look at it. So far, she'd succeeded in refusing.

But for how long? She might be good at solving puzzles, but she was pretty sure this was one she didn't dare tackle.

CHAPTER SIX

SANTI WAS LOOKING through papers when a knock sounded at his door. Sasha, who'd been lying under his desk at his feet, got up and looked toward the door, her tail wagging. She was wearing a pink tutu around her midsection. He hoped Tomás liked her. He glanced at the sports watch on his wrist. Just before six. It had to be Elena coming to ask about their visit with the teen. *"Entra."*

He motioned for the dog to sit just as the door swung open using the automatic system they all had on the wall. And, yes, it was Elle.

Sasha ducked her head under the desk to look, still sitting exactly where Santi had told her to.

"You're not afraid of dogs, right?"

"No. Why? Are you hiding one?"

He murmured to Sasha, who ran around the desk and sat beside Elle's chair.

"Oh, my goodness! I love her. Is it all right if I pet her?"

"Yes, absolutely. She'd be hurt if you didn't."

While she stroked the dog's head, Santi glanced at her. Today she was dressed in a long beige skirt that had a kind of purposeful crinkling. Her top was a white button-down that had to be murder outside in the heat. But here in the air-conditioning, it was fitted and crisp and molded over some features he was doing his best not to glance at, especially as she leaned over to take Sasha's proffered paw. But it was tricky, as in virtually impossible. His eyes moved to her wrists and fingers, which were devoid of jewelry, and her feet, which had on pumps today rather than sandals.

"Have you taken her to see Tomás yet?"

He frowned. "No, I thought we were doing that together."

"Oh, we are. But I thought you might have peeked in on him before I got here. I was running a little late. And that ballet skirt is adorable on her."

"The kids seem to like it. And no, I haven't peeked in. I just got here a few minutes ago myself. Did you hear that Patricia Gomez is awake and set to be discharged soon?"

"Grace called me before I left the house and told me. That's great news. Any idea exactly what caused it? I heard it was auto-immune related."

With a sigh, Sasha plopped down at Elle's feet, making her smile.

"Yes. They're doing some more tests. So far they haven't narrowed it down, but I'm sure Dario will explore all of his options."

Right on cue, Elle's face colored slightly. Had the man texted her again? She said it had been Grace who called her. Besides, what business of his was it? Hell, even if she wanted to date the man it was of no con-sequence to him.

She didn't have to worry about any of that with him. He had no interest in dating any-one. He'd had exactly two one-night stands with women since Carmen's death. Totally about physical release. The women hadn't wanted anything further, either, which had made it perfect.

He hated to admit it, but Elle would have

been his third encounter in those six years, if that kiss had gone any further than it had. But this weird sense of homecoming had flooded his system the second their lips collided. It had made him yank away from her. And thank heavens he had or working with her would have been…impossible. He was already highly aware of her this afternoon, maybe because of their talk yesterday. He had a feeling she didn't get asked about her riding all that often and the fact that she'd opened up about it had made something in his chest turn all soft.

Soft? It wasn't only his chest that was going soft. His brain evidently was, too. He needed to pull himself together. And fast.

"Are you ready to go see him?"

She nodded. "Any other thoughts on what's causing his leg pain?"

"Not yet. You?"

"I'm still going through some lists of differentials. Blood clots in the femoral being one of them, but there would have to be one on each side and only partially obstructing the vessels. The chances of that happening are…"

"Infinitesimal."

"Exactly. One of the dystrophies, like we mentioned earlier?"

He thought about that for a minute. Becker's was a possibility, although it didn't normally present with pain. But if Tomás was trying to force his muscles past any perceived weakness, there could be some soreness involved afterward. "Yes, there are a couple that come to mind for this age range. Becker's and Duchenne's."

"Ugh. Those are both catastrophic diagnoses." Her voice was soft and there was a sadness he hadn't expected.

"Yes, they are." If anyone knew about catastrophic diagnoses, it was Santi. He remembered the moment he and Carmen had received her diagnosis: stage four breast cancer that had spread to her brain and left femur. She'd actually gone in for leg pain and after a slew of tests, they found it was metastatic cancer originating in her breast.

"Those are both caused by recessive genes. We don't have any history on the parents, if I remember right."

"No. The home said there's nothing other than the notes from his heart surgeries. There are normally some abnormalities on

EKGs found on initial workup with Becker's, but since he's had the Fontan procedure for his hypoplastic left heart syndrome, his EKGs and echoes are abnormal, even on a good day. In other words, the findings might be so unremarkable they might not show up."

"Urine?" She glanced over at the wall. "Mind if I use that?"

He followed her gaze where a large whiteboard was hung. On it were a few notes from another meeting. "Feel free to erase all of that."

"Are you sure?"

He nodded, watching as she wheeled her way to the board. Realizing she wouldn't be able to reach the upper portion, he got up and erased it. "Do you want me to write at the top?"

Sasha stayed where she was, but lifted her head to look at them, tail thumping on the ground.

"No, I normally start at the very bottom. I work my way up as far as I can reach. I'll add more once we go see him. But I'd just like to know what to rule out when we head over there."

She wrote the two dystrophies on the lowest part of the board. "Do you have different colors?"

"Let me check." He didn't normally graph things out, but then again, he often referred complicated issues elsewhere. Except they didn't know which specialist Tomás needed. Not yet. He pulled out several of his desk drawers, giving a sigh of relief when an unopened pack of dry-erase pens came into sight.

He took them over and handed them to her. Their fingers accidentally touched, and they both froze for a second, and raw sensation spiraled up his arm and sizzled through his chest. He let go of the pack in a hurry. Unfortunately she chose to do the same and the box of markers dropped onto the ground.

"Demonio!" The swear word slipped out before he could stop it. He swooped down to pick up the box and his head collided with something on his way down.

"Ouch!" Elle's yelp caught him up short, and he almost bumped into her again.

Sasha leaped up and he had to reassure her, patting her silky head.

He was about to apologize to Elle, when

the diagnostician suddenly giggled, hand going to cover her mouth. Then she laughed harder, her palm moving from her mouth to the back of her head, rubbing it.

Santi started to voice that apology, but there was something about those little chortles that were contagious. He found himself chuckling along with her.

It took an effort to shut his laughter down. He looked at her. Really looked. Her cheeks were pink, eyes bright with mirth, and those lips were curved at a luscious angle that made him want to... Before he could stop himself, he leaned over and kissed her softly on the mouth before moving away again.

Some familiar emotion flooded his chest and flared outward, catching him off guard just as her eyes went wide.

"What was that for?" she asked.

He had no idea. It had been an impulsive move, almost as if it was muscle memory. Then he realized why, and he damned himself. He'd often done that with Carmen.

Santi swallowed and made something up. "I think I just needed a reason to laugh today.

It's been a hard few shifts with Tomás's condition hanging over my head."

"Yes, it has. Speaking of hard and heads." She fingered Sasha's pink tutu, avoiding his eyes. "Has anyone told you that you have a very hard head?"

"Hmm, let's see… My mother, various teachers, my coworkers, a couple of friends—"

She held up a hand, smiling. "You can add me to your evidently very long list."

"You got it." He handed her the pack of pens, careful not to touch her this time. Having her here in his office was doing things to his libido that he didn't like. Especially since the moon was just starting to appear within sight of his window, reminding him that their meetings were almost always at night. Working these shifts was partly about not having to go to bed at night and tossing and turning at being there alone.

Somehow it was easier for him to sleep during the day. It also helped him manage any interactions with women, since they were normally sleeping when he was working and working when he was sleeping. No dinner dates. No movie nights. No complications. His job was perfect in that respect.

Except the one woman he'd kissed in ages now worked the exact same hours he did. In the same place. And it was getting harder and harder to not let his thoughts travel in that direction.

He glanced again at the darkening sky before turning his attention back to her.

She'd pulled out red and green felt tip pens and had added some of the diagnostic markers above each condition. Then listed the tests they needed to either confirm or rule out whether Tomás met those markers.

"What else?"

"We'd mentioned multiple sclerosis. He's young but…no, scratch that. The CT scan didn't show any suspicious lesions."

"Right. Which rules out brain tumor as well, and some other problems."

Together they thought up and either ruled out or added other conditions to their board. He could have a problem with bone lesions in his legs, but to have those bilaterally would be as odd as bilateral blood clots.

Elle sighed. "Maybe the most important thing is figuring out how to get him to open up to us."

"I know. I'm hoping Sasha will be some

help, but if not, we may need to pull in some reinforcements in the form of counselors who are trained to deal with this." Not that Santi had gone to anyone after his wife died, despite friends urging him to do just that. But opening up had never been one of his better traits.

Evidently it wasn't one of Tomás's, either.

"I'm hoping he'll just start to trust us."

Santi realized they were sitting with their heads close together. Too close. All he had to do was look over at her and their faces would be inches apart.

As if she were having similar thoughts, Elle suddenly capped the pens and put them back in the box. "Let's go see him."

She took out her phone and snapped a picture of the board for reference. "I assume Sasha's outfit is for Tomás's benefit."

"How do you know she doesn't just like to dress up?" He had no idea why he suddenly felt so carefree, especially when he was about to see a child who could have a life-threatening condition in addition to his rerouted circulatory system. But that quick kiss and the sense of intimacy being so close had engendered had somehow given him a burst of energy. For now, he was just going to sit back and enjoy it. He could worry about the ramifications later on.

And Elle hadn't seemed to mind the impulsive move. He almost wished she'd have shut him down immediately. Instead, she'd seemed almost bright. Almost as…

No. He wasn't happy. Wasn't glad. And that kiss wasn't happening again. He climbed to his feet.

"Come on, Sasha. Let's go." He clipped a lead onto the pink harness that matched the tulle around her waist, and they headed out the door and down the hall.

As they got closer to his room, Tomás's shrill voice echoed down the hallway, causing Sasha to balk.

Santi hurried ahead and found a representative of the group home in the room with the teen. "I'm sure you'll be getting out of the hospital soon," the woman said.

"I don't want to!" His face was beet red, a dangerous sign.

The woman tried to calm him down, but the more she cajoled and pleaded, the more agitated he seemed to become.

Before he could put a stop to the exchange, Elle moved forward and smiled at the woman. "Can I talk to you outside for a moment?"

"Of course." The poor woman looked relieved, her eyes skipping across Santi's dog. Elle gave him a very tiny nod, telling him to go for it.

He hadn't had much luck yesterday, but he was willing to try again. He moved inside with the Labrador retriever. "How are you doing today, Tomás?"

"Same as every day. I hurt." His voice still held a thread of anger, but his gaze was glued to Sasha. "Is that the dog you were telling me about?"

Rather than sullen, today the teen sounded resigned as if he didn't expect anything different now. "Yes, this is Sasha. Is it okay if she comes closer?"

The boy shrugged but swung his legs over the side of the bed, wincing as he did.

"Let me lower the bed a bit, so you can say hi to her." He stepped on a mechanism at the side of the frame and the hydraulics whispered as the bed moved downward.

"Why is she wearing a dress?"

He looked at his pup. "It's not really a

dress. It's kind of that poufy part on a ballet costume."

Tomás blinked. "Does she dance?"

"No. She just tries to make people feel better."

The boy sat there for a minute. "Huh. People like me, you mean."

Santi didn't try to dodge the comment. "Yes, people just like you. And people like me." He held the dog away just a touch. "Do you feel strong enough to walk over here?"

Tomás licked his lips. "I don't know." Resting his feet on the ground, he stood, his gait a strange shuffling movement as he made his way toward Sasha. His posture was stooped as if anticipating pain.

"Does it hurt now?"

"Not as bad as it did a few minutes ago." He reached Sasha just as Elena came back into the room. Santi could feel her critical gaze as she watched Tomás's movements. He was pretty sure she was trying to read him.

"Can I pet her?"

"I think she would like that. Curl your fingers into your palm and hold your fist out to her so she can sniff you first."

Tomás did as he was told, and Sasha did

her part by giving a perfunctory sniff before her tongue swiped across his hand.

The teen made a sound that was suspiciously like a squeaked laugh. "She's nice. I wish I could have a dog."

Santi did his best to hide his shock at the softer tones. Maybe this had been the right call after all. If only they could keep the boy like this, they might be able to get somewhere.

"I'm sure when you get a little older you'll be able to. We just have to help you feel better first."

The teen looked down at his feet. "My legs are tired."

Santi glanced as well, and sure enough the muscles in his thighs were shaking. "Let's go ahead and get you back in the bed."

Tomás leaned over to pet Sasha's neck again and all of a sudden cried out in pain, his legs almost crumpling before he caught himself. Sasha remained very still.

Whatever had happened had put him in agony.

"What is it?" Elena moved forward to help him back to the bed, careful to avoid bumping his legs with her chair. "Did it hurt when you stretched down like that?"

Tomás sank onto the bed, his relief evident in his face. "Yes. Just like before when I leaned over to get my shoes."

"Stretch your arms out to the side."

He did as she asked. "Does it hurt now?"

"Not like it did."

She moved around in front of him, her face level with his. "I'm going to ask you to do something, Tomás. And it's very possible it might hurt. A lot."

His features went white, and he looked at Sasha with pleading eyes. He hadn't seemed this vulnerable any of the other times they'd met him. It had to be Sasha's doing.

Elle looked over her shoulder at him. "Can you bring her closer, if she won't be frightened of Tomás making a sound if something hurts."

"She's used to it." Santi didn't want to say that when Sasha was a puppy, she'd heard Carmen cry out in pain many times toward the end of her life.

He moved her closer, and Sasha laid her head on Tomás's knee.

"Okay, Tomás, I want you to curve your

back and lean toward Sasha as if you're going to give her a hug. Do it very, very slowly and stop if it starts hurting at all."

He could almost see her brain picking at the problem as if the answer was right there, she just couldn't quite get to it. He liked that. Liked the way her analytical mind could take things apart and put them back together.

As long as she wasn't analyzing him. Because she could get a little too close to the truth, if she did.

Tomás placed his palm on the dog's head and slowly did what Elle had asked. In micromovements, he curved, bending until he was about a quarter of the way down before suddenly stopping. "It hurts really bad."

"Is the pain burning? Is it stabbing?"

"It burns, and it makes my legs feel funny. Like when they fall asleep."

"Okay, slowly sit back up and tell me if it feels better."

Tomás straightened, his eyes closing as if in relief. "Yes, it feels better, but my legs still hurt."

"Do you still have pins and needles in them?"

"It's kind of going away, but the pain is still pretty bad."

She looked over her shoulder at Santi. "I think I know what it is. And we're going to have to act fast if we're going to save function in his legs."

CHAPTER SEVEN

ELENA WAS 99 percent sure she was right, but they'd need an MRI to be sure.

She'd moved into the hallway with Santi, leaving Sasha in the room with Tomás, who was busy trying to seem like he didn't care, all the while petting the dog's head. Leaving the door open so she could keep an eye on the pair, she kept her voice low. "I think he has a tethered cord. It kind of hid itself while he was small and because of all of the difficulties with his heart, no one thought to look at anything else, especially since it wasn't causing symptoms at the time."

"A tethered cord." He glanced in the room. "It makes more sense than a dystrophy at this point. I think we can rule those out."

"I think so, too. He's hit a growth spurt and the trapped portion of his spinal cord is being stretched. Bending forward like that only stretches it more. It has to be near where the nerves to his legs are centered."

Strangely, Elena felt relief. A tethered cord was serious, no doubt about it. Tomás had been worried about ending up in a wheelchair like she was, and unless surgery was done to free the cord, he may very well be. Some of his impairment might be permanent, but if they could free it, there was a chance they could reverse some of the damage since he hadn't been symptomatic for long.

"Let's schedule an MRI to confirm, and I'll get a hold of the neurology department. Hopefully the cord is simply stuck, probably from a neural tube defect that closed and narrowed the space. If the cord itself is too short, surgery may be more complicated."

She nodded. "Osteotomy to shorten his spine. That would be tougher, but either way he has a great chance at recovery."

"All right. Do you mind staying here with Sasha and Tomás, while I make some calls?"

"I don't mind at all. Do I need to take Sasha's skirt off, or is she okay?"

"It's not tight. She kind of likes the attention she gets from it, I think."

She peered in the door to see the teen actually smiling. *Smiling!* He looked more at ease than she'd seen him in…well, ever.

"Can you call the home as well and let them know? The director was called back to help with something, so she's not here."

"I'll do it."

He went one way, while Elena went back into the room. "How are you doing?"

Glancing up, his smile faded, but so had the angry look he'd carried with him. "Am I going to die?"

"No. We think the problem is in your back and it's causing the pain you're feeling. You'll need surgery, but I think it will help."

"Is that a promise?"

He probably hadn't had many of those that meant much, and Elena wasn't about to heap another one onto the pile.

"Let's not get ahead of ourselves. We need to give you an MRI, kind of like the scan you did a few days ago. We should be able to see on there if it is what I think it is."

"What is it?"

"Something called a tethered cord. Your

spinal cord is trapped somewhere, I think, and we need to free it."

He nodded, appearing to be mulling over what that meant. "So leaning forward pulls on it?"

Her brows went up at how quickly he'd grasped what it meant.

"That's exactly right, Tomás. Surgery can either widen the canal and allow the cord to move freely like it should, or we'll need to help it a little more." She decided to leave the idea of osteotomy for another day. It might not even be necessary.

His head ducked for a minute before his eyes came up and met hers. "Thank you. Can you let Dr. McKenzie know? I… I wasn't very nice to her the last time I saw her."

"I will. It's hard when your body isn't acting like you expect it to. It can make you scared…or angry."

He stroked Sasha's head again. The dog was still sitting in front of the boy looking up at him with adoring eyes. Santi was right. The pup did like her job, and maybe even her costumes. Dressing her up probably signaled she was getting to go somewhere with

Santi. She could see how that might make her happy.

Like Elena getting to go to the hippotherapy center with him? No, it was not like that at all.

She spoke again before she could dwell on those thoughts. "I'm sure Caitlin understands and from what she said to me, she was very worried about you. That's why she asked us to keep trying to figure it out. She got married you know."

"I know. She told me. Does it make you angry that you can't walk?"

The question came out of nowhere, startling her. She answered honestly. "Sometimes, yes. But it's been a long time and I'm happy for the things I can still do."

"Like figure out what's wrong with people?"

She smiled. "Yes, exactly like that."

He paused for a minute or two and glanced at Sasha before speaking again. "Do you think Bianca is mad at me?"

"Bianca?"

He nodded. "She's the *madre* of the home. I wasn't very nice to her, either."

"No, you weren't. But there's always time to tell her you're sorry."

"I will." He took an audible breath. "I'm ready for surgery. As long as Sasha can be there when I wake up."

She wheeled a little bit closer and placed her hand on his, the chilled skin telling her the state of his nerves. This kid had probably been terrified his whole life, using his sullenness as a cover. Actually, she knew he was. She could see it in the way he seemed to be trying to make things right with people before he had surgery. It was another indicator of how scared he was.

And now Tomás had his answer.

And so did she. She blinked as a realization hit her. Finding Tomás's problem meant she'd soon be moving up to the fifth floor, where her real office was. Where Dario Mileno was. She blew out a breath. It also meant she wouldn't be seeing Santi every day.

Did that bother her?

It did. And she wasn't sure why. She'd worked with lots of doctors in her career and had never had any problem moving on.

But those other doctors had never kissed

her. He'd done so twice. Once at the wedding, and that kiss when they'd been laughing in his office. The first one had awoken her senses, trickling desire through her in an agonizing stream. But that second one... Well, it had awoken something far more dangerous than her body. It had stirred her emotions, making them long for something she'd given up on a long time ago: permanent companionship. The touch of lips had been short and playful, but she'd caught a glimpse of what life could look like. And she was having a harder time shaking that off.

She'd still work with him from time to time, once she moved, but probably not as closely as she was now, unless there was another case like this one.

Sasha nosed her hand as if understanding what she was thinking. She stroked the dog's warm soft fur and leaned close to her ear. "Shh, girl. This has to be our little secret."

"What's a secret?"

Tomás had evidently overheard her soft words.

"Yes, what's a secret?" The low gruff voice made her sit up quickly. Santi had walked up behind her with such stealth that she hadn't heard him. Neither had Sasha, evidently, as her head popped off Elena's leg, and she whirled toward her owner, tail wagging.

"That I'm going to put a dog cookie jar in your office and keep it stocked with pup treats." She had no idea how that fib had come out so quickly but was glad it had. Sasha was a great therapist, maybe too good. She'd helped break through some of the walls that Tomás had erected. But not only that, she seemed to see into Elena's deepest hopes. And fears. And she found they were one and the same. She wanted deeper relationships. Desperately. And yet she feared them. So much so that she tended to sabotage any possibility of having one.

"You are, are you?"

Maldición! Now that she'd said it, she was stuck with it. Which meant she would have to come down to his office periodically to fill the jar. Still, she decided to just go with it. "Is that okay? Unless she's on a special diet and can't have them."

"I'm sure she would appreciate having some when she's here."

His voice was slow and there was a hint of something in his tone that she didn't understand. A kind of softness that made her tummy go all wonky. And ignited that fear all over again.

She squashed the emotion, making a mental note to look for a doggy-themed cookie jar the next time she was out. And maybe some of those fancy home-baked treats they sometimes had at specialty cookie shops that were made with canines in mind.

The dog was currently sitting by Santi's side, but Sasha's soft brown eyes were on her, as if to say, "It's okay. Your secret really is safe with me."

It made her smile. "Tomás would like Sasha to be here when he wakes up from surgery, if that's possible—*if* the MRI shows a tethered cord."

"Yes, can she?" The teen's voice was soft, tentative, and it tugged at her heart. She hoped at least one of the foster homes he'd lived in had had a pet that he'd been able to bond with.

But that made it so much harder, didn't it? To bond with an animal—or person, for that matter—only to have them ripped away from you.

Like Santi's wife? There had been a sadness to his voice when he'd talked about her. It was obvious, despite the time that had elapsed since her passing, that he still loved her deeply. Maybe that's why he wasn't currently married, or even in a relationship from what she'd gathered. Some loves were irreplaceable.

She felt that way about Strato. She didn't see him as often as she would like or even as often as she should, but that horse was irreplaceable. He'd tried to move toward her after her fall, almost tugging the reins from her friend's hands. And whenever she'd visited the last couple of times, his majestic neck had curved, and he'd lowered his head to nuzzle her hair, warm breath blowing across her face. She'd held his head against hers and whispered an apology.

He was a talented boy, and he had always liked to work. Probably keeping him had been selfish on her part, but she just couldn't seem to give him up.

Her glance went to Santi.

No! Do not attach those kinds of feelings to him. To anyone. Hadn't Renato taught her that? Or the fact that she hadn't had a real relationship since then? People left. Her boyfriend from high school hadn't stuck around long once he realized her injuries were permanent. His sheepish expression the last time he visited had told her all she needed to know. The football jock had loved to brag that she was as good in her sport as he was in his. His sliding away had been awful and a terrible blow to her self-esteem on top of her other struggles. She'd gone through a depression that had taken months to work through. Renato not calling her after their failed lovemaking attempt had been just as much of a blow.

"Sasha won't be allowed in recovery or ICU, where you'll probably be when you first come out of surgery, but we can do a video chat with her on the line. How's that?"

Santi's voice jerked her back to reality.

She'd totally forgotten that she'd asked the question. Not good. Her thoughts were ricocheting around like those polo balls Santi probably batted when he was playing. Or did he even play here?

Glancing over, she noted the slight strain of muscles against his black polo shirt and the trim abs. He said he didn't ride as much as he'd like, but from the look of him, he found some way to exercise. He was strong and in shape.

Of course he jogged, as she'd seen that day in the park.

"That's okay." Tomás held his hand out, and Sasha immediately padded over to him in her pink tutu, soaking up the attention.

Yes, the dog deserved a treat jar. And a medal.

Maybe she should look into getting a dog.

"Did you get a hold of neurology?" she asked.

"Yes. They've had several emergency surgeries over the last forty-eight hours, so they're backed up a bit. But we'll get the MRI, and they'll take a look. If it confirms tethered cord syndrome, they'll work you in, Tomás, in the next couple of days."

Elena reached up to give the boy's shoulder a slight squeeze. "It won't be much longer, and you'll be feeling better."

The teen looked away for a long minute, before saying, "I really thought I was going to die."

Santi looked at her and she knew exactly what his thoughts were. That Tomás hadn't opened up this much the whole time they'd been working with them.

Tomás had probably faced dying many times in his life, with his heart. And he would probably face it again sometime in the future. The fortunate thing was that if the Fontan circulation started to fail, he was young and healthy enough to go on the transplant list.

"This is definitely a better scenario than some of the other possibilities," she said.

Surgery would be complicated by his heart problems, but it certainly wasn't an insurmountable obstacle.

"Okay, Sasha, time to say goodbye so Tomás can get prepped for his MRI," Santi said. He glanced at her and the teen. "Neurology has already got you scheduled. They should be here soon to take you up. And I'll check on you a little later in the evening."

Tomás nodded and started to lean over, arms stretched wide, to hug Sasha, before stopping himself. She knew why he'd hesitated, and her heart ached over it. Soon, though, he wouldn't have to worry about pain when reaching to give hugs to the dog…or to anyone. She gave an inner sigh.

And that was a very good thing. It made everything, even her confusion about Santi, worth it.

Santi fed Sasha her afternoon meal and took her for a quick walk outside his apartment. Although he didn't live in the hospital housing complex, he did run in the park regularly after work. He still did. He hadn't come across Elena while doing so since that first morning, and he wondered if she'd chosen to run at another time to avoid him, or if it was just his screwed-up mind inserting things that shouldn't be there. He couldn't believe he'd kissed her in his office. It was impulsive and stupid, and while he might not always be the smartest human alive, one thing he prided himself on was not being impulsive.

And yet he had been.

So why Elena?

He didn't know, and he didn't care. But one thing he didn't want to do was sit around and brood while eating a meal in front of the television. Making a quick call to Javier and Caitlin, he told them what Elena had figured out with Tomás. How quickly she'd figured it out still amazed him. That woman's mind worked in ways he couldn't begin to fathom.

"A tethered cord? I never even thought of that," Javier said. They were on speakerphone so they both could hear and talk.

"I didn't, either. Elle did, though. You were right about her figuring the hard ones out, Caitlin."

"So it's Elle now, is it?" Her voice contained a hint of slyness that Santi didn't like. He didn't want anyone getting any ideas. "We all use first names at Aelina, you know that. It would be awkward to call her Dr. Solis and everyone else by their given names."

"I'm just teasing, Santi. Javier, how do you say 'take a chill pill' in Spanish?"

"Toma un tranquilizante."

Caitlin laughed. "Well, that certainly fits. What Javier said, Santi."

Take a tranquilizer? Seriously? In the background he could swear he heard them kissing, and it made his jaw set hard, a muscle pumping in his cheek. "Well, I won't hold you up. When are you coming back to Barcelona?"

"Grace and Diego are having a renewal

ceremony coming up on the beach. We wouldn't miss it for the world."

Maldizion! Not another wedding. Technically Grace and Diego were already married, but they'd had some rocky times. He'd witnessed some of their frosty encounters firsthand. Evidently those days were over, something he'd missed. He forced himself to say something nice. "That's great. I'm glad they've worked out their problems."

"They have. Grace has already said she wants you there along with our other friends. She's going to ask Elena as well. You'll go, won't you? I think she'd be sad if you didn't."

"Since I haven't been invited yet, I'll cross that bridge when it comes."

Javier broke in. "I think our dinner reservations are soon, *querida*."

"Okay, I think he's telling me to get off the line, Santi. See you at the ceremony."

"See you when you get back." He left off anything that might hint at a promise on his part. If he could, he was going to make sure he had something scheduled whenever that beachfront ceremony was. Especially if Elena was going.

He shoved the phone in his pocket. He

definitely didn't want to sit around the house until his shift started. So, Boomers it was. The place was fashioned after the American sports bar model, and he found he liked the noise the place afforded. There were large screens facing every direction and it would give him something to look at besides what was in his own head.

He gave his dog a quick rub, and when she whined, he shook his head. "Sorry, girl. You can't see Tomás tonight. But I promise, you will again soon."

He wondered if the diagnostician had already moved her things up to the fifth floor, or if she was still in her office in pediatrics. She wasn't even officially assigned to the night shift, they'd just put her there to help with Tomás, and since he worked nights, he assumed Letizia from HR had asked her to work during that time frame as well. Soon someone else would claim her as their own.

Okay, that was a weird way to put it, even for him. Maybe it was the memory of Dario's behavior around her. Or the veiled attempts at flirting in his texts to her.

Something about her being around him every single day just didn't sit right. *Mal-*

dizion! He definitely needed to go somewhere besides his apartment.

Heading out the door, he went the short distance from his house to the sports eatery, which was located at about the halfway point to Aelina. He normally biked to work, only using his car when he took Sasha with him, to save her from having to walk on the burning pavement. And he'd drive on Friday as well, when he was taking a small group of kids to On Horses' Wings. And he'd invited Elle, too. Probably not a smart idea after all.

Caitlin was right. The shortened version of the diagnostician's name came to mind far too easily. But to suddenly switch to Elena now would draw attention, and that was the last thing he wanted or needed.

Pushing through the entrance to Boomers, he saw the place was already packed. Although Spaniards tended to eat dinner later than some of its neighboring countries, he needed to be at work, so he'd gotten into the habit of dining earlier. One of the wait staff asked how many were in his party and when he said one, he could swear the woman's smile contained more than a hint of pity.

Who cared? He'd eaten by himself lots of times.

As they walked between tables a voice called out to him. His head turned toward the sound and his stomach dropped. It was Grace.

And Elena.

Great. Just what he didn't need tonight.

He nodded and gave half a wave, hoping to walk on by, but it wasn't to be.

"Join us!"

Glancing at Elena, he saw her head was down, and she was avoiding looking at him, almost as if she felt guilty about something. Had they been talking about him?

It didn't matter if they were. As long as she didn't develop some sort of crush on him. And by the looks of it, there was absolutely no chance of that.

He hesitated a minute, considering his options. If he declined the invitation, it would look odd. But he also wasn't in the mood for awkward, stilted conversation.

Would Elle think the refusal was because of her?

That made his mind up. He motioned toward the table and the server asked him what he wanted to drink. He gave his order and moved over to where the two women sat.

Grace smiled as he took his seat. "We were just talking about the renewal ceremony. You heard about it, didn't you? And of course we want you there."

"I actually called Javier and Caitlin to discuss a patient, and they mentioned that you and Diego were having one. Congratulations. I'll have to check my schedule."

Her head cocked. "I haven't even told you when it is yet."

"I realize that," he lied. "Can you tell me, and I'll look?"

She grinned. "Elena is coming, of course. It's on the twenty-third, two weeks from this coming Friday."

He took his phone out and put the date into it. How was it that he'd not only been stuck going to one wedding, but now it looked like it would be two? All in the course of a month.

A little voice whispered, *Two weddings for two kisses.*

And if there were a third wedding? Would there be another kiss?

He turned his head toward the diagnostician, who was finally looking at him. "Are we still on for this Friday?"

"I have it on my calendar."

Grace smiled. "The On Horses' Wings trip? Elle was just telling me about it. I've been meaning to go to one of the informational meetings and check it out. And now that things between me and Diego are settled, I can finally think about something else."

Elle's teeth came down on her lip and squeezed into it.

So they *had* been talking about him. And he understood exactly what Grace meant. He'd been having trouble thinking of much outside of a certain doctor. And that needed to change. And soon.

"Have you moved up to the fifth floor yet?" The question came totally out of left field, and he was pretty sure it was because of his thoughts about Dario.

Elena blinked. "Oh, um, not yet. I thought I would wait until Tomás was out of the woods in case there's a complication." She hesitated. "Unless you want me to make the move before then."

Maldicion! There was a weird look on her face. He hadn't meant to make her feel unwanted. She wasn't. The fact was, she was "wanted" far too much for his own good. With her dark wavy locks loose and free and looking far too touchable today, he'd needed to say something. Unfortunately it had been the wrong thing.

"No, of course not. I just know you've been working the night shift to help me with Tomás and didn't want you to feel stuck with our vampirish hours."

"I don't feel stuck. And I've actually come to like working at night." She smiled, her tongue coming forward to touch one of her canines. "Do these look longer to you?"

He laughed, despite his earlier thoughts. "Maybe just a touch."

A real smile appeared. He liked it.

"Anyway, if one of the day-shift doctors needed my help, I could swap over and work then instead. My specialty encompasses internal medicine, so I can see patients in my own right as well, so the hospital's money won't be wasted when there are no complicated cases. I just like those cases, which is why I traveled from hospital to hospital before."

"And if you find working so-called easy cases too dull, will you leave Aelina?"

Grace broke in. "We don't want you to leave. So we'll be sure to throw plenty of interesting stuff your way. Right, Santi?"

Hell, he'd done it again. Said the wrong thing. All because *he* was the one who was uncomfortable. He wanted to pull out the sutures of conversation that were unraveling and start again, but unlike with a patient, he couldn't go back and rework things. He was stuck with what he'd said, unless he pulled her aside later and clarified. Which maybe he needed to do.

"Right. I'm sure we can find lots of reasons to keep her here."

When Elle's shoulders visibly relaxed, he knew he'd finally said the right thing.

He decided to add to that. "You are welcome to stay in your office in pediatrics for as long as you'd like. I'm sure our department will have patients you can work with. Or you can just have your base camp set up there and rove from floor to floor, rather than hospital to hospital."

"Thanks, I appreciate that."

Grace smiled. "Santi is head of pediatrics, so he calls the shots there. So if he says you stay, you stay."

"Good to know."

Santi added, "That doesn't mean I'm your boss, though."

He wasn't sure why he felt that additional bit of information was needed. Maybe because he didn't want her to think those kisses were from a superior and that she was expected to play along. If he kissed her, he wanted her to kiss him back because she wanted to, not because she felt her job was in jeopardy.

If he kissed her?

Santi needed to get control of himself and fast. He wasn't sure what was going on with him, but this train was beginning to pick up speed. And it wasn't just the normal city-to-city train that meandered along making plenty of stops. One where he could hop off at any time. No, this was a bullet train that didn't stop until it reached its final destination. Which was what? Sex? A relationship?

Carmen's death had almost destroyed him. He couldn't afford to let anyone else get under his skin again. Because losing someone else, either to death or something else, might just be the end of him.

CHAPTER EIGHT

FRIDAY CAME FAR too soon, and Elena was nervous. Really nervous. She hadn't been around horses other than Strato since her accident, and she was halfway afraid it would pull all those memories of pain and despair back to the surface. She remembered doctors telling her how lucky she was that her spinal cord wasn't completely severed.

Lucky. She hadn't thought so.

At first that news had given her a burst of hope that maybe her damaged nerves would find new pathways, and she'd be able to go about her life as she'd done before the accident. From her hospital bed, she read everything she could find on spinal cord injuries. But the more information she took in, and the more time that went by, the more despair she felt. She might have some feeling in her left leg, but once six months hit, she knew it was less and less likely she'd have any miraculous advances.

She tried her hardest during physical therapy, pushing herself beyond her limits, until her doctors talked to her parents, who in turn urged her to slow down, telling her she was going to do more damage to herself.

So with her extra time, she studied. And she studied. And she studied. The doctors on her case were amazed by the amount of information she had amassed in such a short time and the way her brain worked through and retained minute details. One of them suggested she might want to study medicine.

Somehow that resonated. She wanted to be involved in hard cases, cases like hers. The cases where patients needed hope. She might not be able to give it to them, but she would work her ass off trying to find answers. If there was a treatment, she wanted to be the one who helped figure it out.

It was why when Tomás stretched for Sasha and it hurt, her brain immediately tried to sift through the possible explanations.

Now that she was at a permanent location

and would be dealing with patient exams on a regular basis, she'd been toying with adding a third wheelchair to her group. One that had the feature of a hydraulic system that would lock her legs and hips in and lift her to a standing position. With that, she could examine patients more efficiently. And since she'd retained some use of her left hip and leg, if her ankle and knee could be braced, she could manage it a little more easily, even though those chairs were designed for people who were fully paraplegic.

She purposely did not wear breeches today, opting for pants that would be totally unsuitable for riding, just so no one thought she was eager to get on. She wasn't. Strato was her heart horse, and she couldn't imagine another equine taking his place. If she couldn't ride him... Well, she wasn't going to ride. And she knew that her lack of confidence would be transferred to any horse she was on, and horses—being a prey animal and living in a herd—needed a confident leader in order to feel safe.

They were taking the hospital's van, which was equipped with a chair lift, another of their attempts at accessibility. Santi was going to get the children and then swing by her apartment. Doing a last swoosh of mascara and checking her hair, she declared herself ready. Well, not ready, but as ready as she'd ever be.

Almost as soon as she exited the bathroom, her doorbell rang. She closed her eyes. Here it was. The moment of truth.

And if she couldn't hold it together?

She would somehow force herself to remain calm. The last thing she wanted anyone to find out was how very much she missed her horse. Missed riding. Missed her old life.

Making her way to the door, she opened it and found Santi there. He'd exchanged his normal khakis and polo shirt for dark washed jeans that hugged his frame and a rust T-shirt emblazoned with the name of the hippotherapy center. The color brought out the dark tan of his skin and made her struggle to normalize her breathing. And the thought of him volunteering to help people who needed it brought a lump to her throat.

He did that on a daily basis through his job, but this was different. This showed how deeply he loved kids. How much he wanted them to have a good life. This man would make an amazing father, if he'd allow himself to love again.

She had no idea why that thought had popped into her head.

"Hi," she said, her voice a little breathier than she would have liked.

"Hello, yourself. Are you ready?"

"I am."

They just stood there for a minute, neither of them talking, then Santi seemed to realize they should be moving. He stood aside so she could roll out.

Her purse was already slung across the back of her chair. She had her own wheelchair-accessible van, but since the hospital was so close, she rarely used it. There was even a small grocery store located a couple of blocks away, which made it nice. All in all, it was the ideal place to settle down.

If it weren't for her weird attraction to Santi that she just couldn't seem to shake. And thinking about him rocking a child in his arms? That was definitely off-limits.

She got in the van, and they were off. There was eager chatter all around her as three little girls were excitedly talking about seeing horses. She smiled when one of the kids, who was also in a wheelchair, craned her neck to look at her.

"Do you have any stickers on your chair?"

When Elena glanced at the girl's ride, she saw there were stickers from seemingly everywhere she'd been. From animal parks to amusement parks, her chair told a story of what the child liked and places she'd been. Her friend Letizia's chair was similar.

"I don't, but that's a good idea. I like yours a lot."

"Me, too. My mom helps me put them on."

Speaking of moms. There were no parents in the van, so they must trust Santi and the hospital quite a bit to let him take their kids on this outing. And he was comfortable enough around kids to not feel the need for extra support. Or maybe that's what she was here for. She didn't think so, though. It was more like he knew she'd ridden in the past and thought she might want to ride again someday.

She guessed she should have been clearer that she wasn't looking to reenter equestrian activities. Not yet.

If not now, then when? She wasn't getting any younger.

Thirty-two is hardly ancient, Elle.

No, but she wanted to do it on her own terms. Just like in the romance department. Trusting herself to anyone at this juncture was a scary prospect. If it turned out like Renato or her high school boyfriend… Yeah, not something she saw herself doing anytime soon.

It took about fifteen minutes to reach the center. It was beautiful. A big Spanish-style barn with clay roofing tiles and stuccoed block walls, it was geared to stay cool in the heat of the summer. On the front of the building was a hand-painted tile sign. At the top, it read En Alas de Caballo. Just below the name of the center was a watercolor depiction of a child in a wheelchair seated next to a horse, a currycomb in her hand. Next to that appeared the words *Healing Comes in Many Forms.*

She swallowed. It was true. There was physical healing, but there were also many other kinds. Her emotional and psychological healing had taken much longer than that of her physical injuries. And in some ways, it was an ongoing process, even now.

"Okay, everyone ready?"

That was her cue to say no she wasn't, right? There was no way she could do that in front of kids who were chattering about the opportunity to see actual horses. Instead of excitement, though, all she felt was dread.

"Do we get to see your horse?"

Santi smiled. "Actually yes, Billy will be the horse they'll bring in. You'll all get a turn to brush him and pet him. Sound good?"

A cheer went up.

So Santi had told these children about the horse he'd put into the therapy program?

Looking at him, he didn't seem tense about seeing the horse again. Of course, he did say he volunteered at the center, so he got to be with Billy on a regular basis.

Her heart cramped for a second, thinking of Strato and how few times she'd seen him. She made a note to fly to Mallorca the next vacation she had and see her old friend.

Santi got out along with two of the girls, went to the right side of the van and opened the door to the lift, sending it up. He called in to her. "Elle, do you mind helping Margarita get her chair locked into the lift and sending her down?"

She blinked. Not at his shortening her

name—which she liked far too well—but at the simple request. She was so used to people being overly accommodating, trying to do things for her that she could do herself, that she was surprised he'd asked her to do anything.

A whoosh of emotion threatened to overwhelm her and their eyes locked for a second. Then two. She had to look away or risk being lost in the warm depths of his irises. It was on the tip of her tongue to thank him, but she didn't want to make things strange, so she smiled instead, forcing a lightness into her voice that she didn't feel. "I'll be happy to."

She went over and had to stretch to unlock the mechanism on the floor that held the girl's chair in place.

"You're very pretty." The girl's voice was quiet and shy, just like it had been when they'd talked about the stickers on her wheelchair.

"Why, thank you, Guida," she said, the nickname coming instinctively as she'd heard other girls call the child that. "I think you're very pretty, too."

Guida rolled over to the lift and expertly

backed herself in. She'd been doing this for a while, if not her whole life. "Okay, I'm ready."

Elena locked her in and then pressed the button.

"See you at the bottom," the girl said.

That made her smile. Maybe this trip wouldn't be as terrible as she'd feared. After all, she could focus on the girls and their excitement and let it carry her through whatever horse stuff she'd be required to do.

Santi helped the girl out and sent the lift back up.

This van was slightly different from hers, but it was still fairly easy for her to reach everything. She got in and then pushed the button for it to move to ground level, even though Santi also had a set of controls on the side of the vehicle.

There was a slight bump as it reached the bottom, and he pulled the door open, waiting for her to wheel out. She smiled up at him and he gave her shoulder a slight squeeze that sent goose bumps over her.

His touch made her react in weird ways. Even as he walked beside her toward the door to the center, his hand grazing her upper arm from time to time, accidentally she was sure. But he didn't seem nearly as bothered by those soft brushes as she was.

He pushed a buzzer and identified himself to the voice that came through the speaker. "Hi, it's Santi here with my group."

A mechanism clicked, allowing the door to be opened. He reminded the kids that they couldn't yell or scream or run around the horse. "We have to be very calm, so we don't startle him."

Even though he'd said Billy was a very quiet horse, any equine could be startled and react in unexpected ways. She'd had Strato spook on her any number of times. But at least most of those times she'd kept her seat. And when she had fallen, she'd been able to leap up and continue her ride. Except for that last time.

The tension built again as they entered the building and reached a riding arena that contained a spectator area as well as the place where the actual interaction with the horses would take place.

"This is a little different from traditional hippotherapy, which involves one-on-one treatment of a patient using a horse. Here there are multiple clients in each class. Most of our center's instructors are certified physical therapists who are also certified in the equine portion of the spectrum. It's quite an involved process."

Since Elena knew almost nothing about equine therapy programs, what he'd said kind of went over her head, but she could understand that different programs had different affiliations. At least she assumed they did.

A woman came out of a side door, and she and Santi exchanged traditional Spanish air kisses. The woman was beautiful, with long dark hair, and unlike Elena, she was clad in skin-tight riding breeches that showed off the curve of her hips and backside.

She touched Santi's arm. "So good to see you outside of class time, Santi. And you brought quite the contingent along with you." Her eyes skimmed over the group, pausing on Elena for a moment. "A new student?"

Suddenly she felt ridiculous in her dress pants. She should have at least worn jeans, even if she didn't want to wear breeches. "No, I'm just here as a visitor." She wanted to head off any questions as to her interest in the program.

She only realized how sharply she'd answered when the woman apologized. Great. She was not only dressed inappropriately, she'd evidently turned into a mean girl as well. "It's okay," she said. "I was injured in a riding accident years ago."

"Well, I hope you enjoy your visit." Unlike Elena, the woman who'd been introduced as the program head was nice in a way that was genuine and not artificial. For some reason, it made Elena like her even less.

It's because of Santi. The thought flitted by before she had a chance to stop it.

She was pretty sure he didn't have a girlfriend. He didn't seem the type to kiss someone if he were involved with someone else. But Elena was also fairly certain that the center's program head had a soft spot for the pediatrician. And who could blame her? He was handsome and kind and caring and loved children. All of the things that most women would leap at.

But Elle wasn't even sure she wanted children, at this point. Not that it was something she dwelled on a lot. Oh, she liked kids.

And Tomás's case had certainly tugged at her heartstrings, but to carry one inside her body? She pushed the thought away when something twinged inside her.

Her parents would certainly love grand-kids, and since she was an only child…

She turned her attention back to the tall woman whose name was evidently Andrea. She was talking about horses and some safety precautions they needed to take. Like not walking behind the horse they were going to bring out in a few minutes.

"Every time a horse takes a step, it acti-vates motor neurons in our bodies. And with each movement he makes, it shifts you, too, so that it's almost like *you're* walking and not the horse. Isn't that cool?"

The girls all nodded.

Great, she was not only gorgeous, she also had mad people skills. Why wouldn't Santi find her attractive? He'd be crazy not to.

Glancing at him, though, she found his eyes weren't on Andrea, they were on her.

Her face turned hot, and she quickly shifted her attention back to the woman in front of them who was demonstrating how to use different brushes and telling them why they were used in the order they were.

"Okay, so are we ready to meet Billy?"

A chorus of yeses went up from the three little girls.

So they really were going to use Santi's horse. What breed had he said he was? Criollo? Or was it just that the horse was similar to one? She couldn't remember.

Suddenly she was curious about Santi's life in Argentina and what his horse would look like.

Andrea sent a text to someone. A minute later, a man entered leading a horse that was shorter than she expected. Probably two hands shorter than her Strato.

But what the horse lacked in height, he made up for in muscle, judging from his wide body and broad chest area. She could see why they were popular with polo players. She assumed they were also used with cattle and livestock. Strato was tall, with long legs and a very sleek body. He was elegant and beautiful. What Billy lacked in elegance he made up for in his kind eyes and ears that were already seeking out the children in front of him. He liked his job. That much was obvious.

The man stopped with the horse toward the front of the arena, a gate standing between the girls and the animal.

Andrea again went over how they needed to approach Billy. "I'm going to let you curry him, one at a time. We'll go through all of the brushes, keeping our hands near the center of his barrel." The man stepped beside the horse and ran his hand over the area they would work on.

She nodded to Santi. "You can go ahead and bring everyone in. If you'll take one child over to Billy and help them brush, Elena and I will stand by the wall in the arena with the rest of the kids, until it's their turn to brush."

"Oh, but…" Her words trailed away. To refuse to participate would seem churlish and would set a terrible example for the kids who were so looking forward to this outing.

Andrea glanced at her as if waiting for her to finish her sentence, but Elena just shook her head.

"Okay, your chairs shouldn't have any problem rolling across the footing, which is shredded tire material. It's cushy on the horse's hooves and is a lot easier for mobility for us humans than moving through sand would be."

They got into the inner sanctum of the arena and Elena found that Andrea was right. It was surprisingly easy to push her chair through the rubber footing, which wasn't deep and was laid over a firm surface. She and Margarita were able to move to where Andrea and the other two girls were waiting.

Santi stood in front of them, legs braced apart, a lime green currycomb in his hand. The color was somehow incongruous with what she knew of him and made her smile. But it somehow just accentuated his strength. His masculinity. She forced herself to swallow. For the millionth time, the word *gorgeous* shimmied through her mind, perking up her nerve endings in a way that was similar to what Andrea had talked about earlier. Only this had nothing to do with the movements of a horse.

"Who wants to go first?" His low tones only threw gasoline onto the smoldering embers in her midsection.

Guida raised her hand more quickly than the other two.

"Okay, let's go. Remember to do everything slowly…quietly." His quick glance at Elena almost made the words sound like they were meant for her.

Fire flared up, licking at everything in its path. She could be pretty damn quiet when she needed to be.

Except he wasn't talking to her, and he certainly wasn't talking about *that*.

Guida was brushing Billy's side, while Santi stood next to the horse, blocking access to the animal's hindquarters without making it obvious that's what he was doing. It was a smart move. He could still interact with the child, while being a physical barrier to anything that might be of danger to her.

Suddenly she wanted to be over there, having Santi standing next to her, pretending to show her what she already knew, his hand covering hers as he showed her how to stroke it across the animal.

Diablos! What was wrong with her? She almost never got like this around men. Not anymore. Not when she'd already seen what a disaster that could be.

Then it was the next girl's turn. She forced her thoughts back to what was happening, listening with half an ear as Guida excitedly told the third child what it was like to stand next to such a large animal, but that Billy looked at her as if telling her that he loved her. "He wanted to help me."

And looking at the Criollo, she thought it might be true. The man at the front still held the horse's lead rope, but there was plenty of slack in its length. Billy was standing there quietly because he wanted to, not because he was forced to.

The last girl was a little more nervous but moved over to where Santi was standing. He explained to her what to do and watched carefully as she brushed the roan horse. And sure enough, Billy turned and looked at the child in a way that she remembered Strato looking at her. As if he could see through to her soul.

That would be a dangerous prospect right now. Because Elena wasn't sure what secrets her soul was carrying. Nothing good, she was sure.

Like the other two girls, he showed her how to use the currycomb, the hard-bristled brush and finally the soft brush that was used for that finishing touch and to flick away any dirt the other brushes might have left behind.

He sent the girl back and moved to the other side of the horse, motioning for Elena to come over.

She started to shake her head no, then remembered she needed to be an example to these girls. To show them that they couldn't let their challenges get the best of them.

Like she'd let them get the best of her in this particular area? Gritting her teeth, she rolled around the front of the horse until she sat beside Billy…and Santi. Probably out of habit, he stood in the same spot he'd been with each child.

Out of a bucket he handed her the curry. "I don't suppose I have to tell you how to use this."

"I think I can remember that much."

She raised the brush and the second she laid her empty hand against Billy's warm side something magical happened. The horse's life and essence seemed to move through her palm and up her arm, carrying something with it.

Healing comes in many forms. The words on the center's sign came back to her. Maybe there really was healing through the touch of a horse.

She began the familiar circular motions of using the curry on Billy, and when she glanced over at him, she caught the wiggle of his bottom lip before he started licking and chewing, a sign of acceptance and understanding in the horse world. She could remember Strato doing the same thing many times as they moved together in the arena. Her horse who loved his work, who was now forced to be a pasture pet, except for the occasional ride that Sandra put on him.

She switched brushes before she was told to, using the hard brush to whisk away the dirt that the curry had raised to the surface. Was it fair to leave Strato in limbo, just because she couldn't ride anymore? The thought caused a pain that was almost unbearable to rise up inside her. She didn't want to give him up. Wasn't sure that she could. And yet he needed activity just like she did to be fulfilled. Maybe some horses were happy with a life of leisure, but she wasn't sure he was.

Billy had a purpose, and from what she saw, he was happy with it. It was there in the forward prick of his ears, the left one swiveling back as he listened for any direction she might give.

Dios, she'd missed this. Missed the touch, the scent of warm skin, the sensation as her finger trailed over shoulder, rib cage and beyond.

She gulped. Was she thinking about horses? Or men?

Santi was watching her, she could feel it, trying to gauge her reaction to Billy. Did she lie and pretend she couldn't stand being here, or did she tell the truth that her joy at being with a horse again was almost unbearable?

The truth. She'd done her best to live by it, no matter how hard that truth was.

She turned with the brush in her hand and looked at the pediatrician. There was an expectancy to his gaze, almost a kind of hope.

"Santi, thank you." She tried to put all the earnestness she could into the words. "I didn't want to come. But I'm so glad I did. I love Billy."

Before she could stop herself, she leaned her right cheek against the horse's side and breathed his scent. The equine's head turned, and warm, soft eyes regarded her with a knowledge that spanned the ages, seeming to know exactly what she'd suffered. Exactly how scared she was to care so much. About him? About Santi? As he blew out a breath, holding very still, she wondered if it even mattered which one. Because maybe… She cared about them both.

And right now—at a stage in her life where she'd come to accept that things weren't going to change for her—that probably was the most terrifying and exhilarating thing she could imagine.

CHAPTER NINE

THE KIDS WERE dropped back off at the hospital and the only ones left in the van were Santi and Elle.

He hadn't been completely sure about pressuring her to go to En Alas de Caballo. But her reaction had blown him away. And when she'd pressed close to Billy's side as if she never wanted to leave, a wave of raw emotion had rolled over him, and for a second it had been hard to catch his breath or control his feelings. He'd started volunteering at the center not long after Carmen's death, afraid if he couldn't find a way to channel his grief into something useful, he would lose himself in a bottle, or worse.

But in all the time he'd been volunteering, nothing had ever moved him as much as Elle's reaction. To the horse. To him. For a second nothing had been hidden. His attraction to her wasn't one-sided. He saw it in her gaze as it moved over the horse. Over him.

But was it smart?

They sat in the van in silence, before he shifted so he could see her in the mirror. She was gazing at him with that same soft, hopeful look he'd seen at the center.

When she looked at him like that, he didn't care about smart. Or anything else.

He debated long and hard about just dropping her back off at her place. But something wouldn't let him.

So he decided to take the plunge and see if what he thought was true actually was.

"Elle, invite me back to your place."

Her teeth came down on her lip, and she hesitated. "Are—are you sure?"

Wasn't that supposed to be his line? But the fear and trepidation in her voice was the same fear she'd had when he'd first asked her to go with him and the kids. And look how that had turned out.

He got out of his seat and climbed back to where she was sitting in the van and squatted beside her chair. Taking her hands in his, he leaned forward and kissed her.

A sharp pang went through him as their lips lingered, as the kiss slowly deepened. His fingers burrowed into the hair at the back of her head, just as her mouth opened.

Dios! He accepted her unspoken invitation, his tongue sliding forward to explore the warm recesses of her mouth. Heat drilled into his chest and began a slow slide toward his lower regions. This van was plenty big to…

No. If this was going to happen, he wanted her in a bed, where he could touch and explore her to his heart's content.

He pulled back, his breathing not quite steady. "Would you like to ask me that question again?"

This time she smiled and leaned forward to kiss him again before saying, "No, I don't want to ask it. And yes, I'd like to invite you back to my apartment. Will you come?"

His thumb and forefinger curled around her chin as his mouth crooked sideways. "Why don't we go and find out. I'm pretty sure I will. Maybe even more than once."

That made her laugh. "Okay, that's not quite what I meant, and you know it."

"Oh, but I couldn't resist." He kissed her again. "I still can't."

"Me, either." She glanced out the window. "But I'd rather get out of the parking lot before someone sees us necking here like two schoolkids."

A quick shadow of something went through him, before he chased it away with a laugh. "Do you want me to drive over to your place?"

"Let's just go through the park, if that's okay? It's not far, and I'd rather the van not be seen parked in front of my apartment."

That was the second time she'd indicated she was worried about them being seen together. Shouldn't he be feeling the same thing?

He surely should. But for the first time in a long time, he didn't really care about anything except getting this woman where he could kiss her some more.

"Okay. The park it is." He forced a smile. "You don't plan on racing me, do you?"

"Afraid you'll lose?"

He was. And it had nothing to do with a race. But that wasn't something he was going to think about right now. He'd been with a couple of women since Carmen had died and had come through the experience pretty much unscathed.

But something was different about this woman. Or was that just his libido talking? He climbed out of the driver's side door and waited for her to use the lift to let herself out. Then he locked up the van and left the keys in the drop box just inside the door of Aelina. He caught up with her just as she was starting on the running path. The sun shone down on her head, making her hair gleam with auburn highlights, and the tip of her nose was pink, probably from her time running her chair up and down the jogging paths in the mornings.

She was gorgeous, but with a vulnerability that he hadn't really noticed until today. She was good at her job, and she knew it. But she had some fears that were probably deep-seated. He'd seen that today at the riding center.

Well, that was okay, because he had some fears, too.

It took about five minutes to get to her apartment, which was the last one in the row of energy-efficient residences. She unlocked the door and pushed it open, motioning for him to go on in. He did, waiting for her to join him and shut the door.

"Do you want anything? A drink?"

No, he didn't. He didn't want anything right now, but her. "I don't. But if you want one, then go ahead."

"No, I don't, either." She seemed to take a deep breath. "I need you to know the last time I tried this with someone, it was a disaster."

He frowned, he had visions of someone hurting her either intentionally or unintentionally and a fire lit in his belly. "Hey, you call all the shots here. If something isn't the way you need it to be, you tell me, okay? If you want me to stop, all you have to do is say the word."

Because by God, he was not going to be the reason she told the next man in her life that their time together had been a disaster. He wanted to make this as good for her as it was going to be for him.

And he already knew it would be good. No matter how it happened, or how this played out. If there was some physical limitation besides her paralysis, they would work it out…find another way. He could think of any number of ways that they could both gain pleasure.

"I don't want to stop. It's just that my legs…"

"Your legs, your arms, your face—everything about you is beautiful and perfect and makes me want you more than I should."

She smiled. "Same."

"I have beautiful legs?" His brows went up.

"Well, I don't know yet, but I'm pretty certain that everything about you is perfect, too." She grinned. "And just for the record, you look really hot in those jeans."

"I do, do I?" He didn't know about hot, but there was a certain amount of heat that was beginning to settle in areas that were going to make themselves known pretty quickly. "Do you need to do anything before I carry you off to bed?"

"You don't have to carry me. I've been getting myself in and out of bed all by myself for a long time."

"This isn't about what you can or can't do. I know you're very capable. But what if I *want* to carry you in there and toss you onto the bed? And kiss you until you can't breathe?"

Her eyes heated. "I think I might like that. I think I might like that very much."

"In that case." He reached down and scooped her into his arms as she gave a little shriek of surprise.

Her arms went around his neck, and she leaned forward to kiss him, planting her lips on his mouth, his chin, nibbling at his jawline. Maybe she'd be the one kissing him until he couldn't breathe, because right now she was doing a pretty good job of lighting his nerve endings on fire.

"Bedroom?"

"Down the hallway, last door on the right."

He carried her, loving the way her fingers toyed with the hair at his nape. Hair that was still a little too long at the moment, but she didn't seem to mind. Those little brushes of warmth against the back of his neck were causing gooseflesh to break out over his arms, his chest. He tightened his grip, finding the door and pushing it open with his shoulder.

Despite his threat of tossing her onto the bed, he instead leaned over and peeled back the covers before setting her down with infinite care, making sure her head was nestled in her pillows. "Okay?"

She shook her head, and a jolt went through him.

"Did I hurt you?"

"No, you're acting like I'm going to break. I won't, you know."

He sat on the edge of the bed and looked down at her, before his finger trailed a course from just under her chin, down her throat, over the swell of one of her breasts.

She gasped, arching up into him in a way that made his cock clench. He wasn't sure exactly where that line of sensation ended, but he intended to find out by the end of their session. But for now... His fingers tunneled under her blouse and bra, finding a nipple, which was already tight and hard. Her eyes closed reflexively before opening again.

As he watched her, his fingers tickled along her rib cage, making her squirm. He liked that: watching her react. He stroked down her belly, ending where her waistband stopped his exploration. "Tell me what you like, *querida.*"

"I like everything. Everything you're doing."

He leaned over and kissed her, letting his lips trail over her features as he unbuttoned her pants and tugged the zipper down. "Wait right there," he whispered against her mouth.

"I'm not going anywhere."

Her breath washed across him, warm and moist and so, so sexy.

As a doctor, he knew all the clinical stuff about paralysis, but every person was different, and he needed to approach things with care. "Anything special that I should know?"

He worked on sliding her pants, admiring her lacy undergarments before hooking his fingers under the elastic and inching those down her legs as well. He felt her shiver when his hand slid down her left thigh.

She waited until he'd gotten her pants off before answering. "I might need some lubrication. It's in the drawer of my nightstand." She hesitated. "And I—I can't sit on you."

His head tilted. Why had she said that? Of course he knew that she couldn't. "I don't expect you to."

"You might not now, but if later you wanted me to try... I—I couldn't."

He got it in an instant. The reason she'd said her last encounter had been a disaster, and he cursed inwardly at the idiot who'd even thought to ask. "I don't need you to, Elle. I just want to love you. This is about both our pleasure, not just mine."

He got the lubricant out of the drawer and laid it on the bed. He then tugged off his jeans, getting a condom out and setting it next to the lubricant.

Her eyes on him were eager, with a hungry look in them that made his insides squeeze together. He recognized that look and it made him swallow back a memory or two of his own. He was not going to let that ruin things for him. For her.

Pulling his shirt over his head, he threw it to the side.

"I was right," she whispered.

His head tilted. "What?"

"You're perfect."

That made him smile. Not so perfect. He stretched out on the bed next to her, still in his briefs. Her shirt had ridden up her smooth belly, laying it bare to his gaze.

He put his palm on it, letting the warmth of her skin seep into him. "You're so incredibly soft." His hand trailed across her, his finger dipping into her belly button. "Can you feel this?"

"Yes." Her voice was breathy with a current of desire that made his body react.

He moved to her right thigh... "Here?"

Her eyes closed. "No, but I can imagine it."

"Where do you want me to touch you?"

"Everywhere. It doesn't matter where I can feel or not feel. I like seeing your fingers running over my body."

"I like that too."

He sat up and slid her shirt up her torso, and she pushed herself up with her arms so he could pull it over her head. Then he reached behind her and undid the clasp on her bra, letting it slide down her forearms.

Unable to resist, he leaned down to take one of her nipples into his mouth, the sweet scent of her skin acting as an aphrodisiac. He pulled, hearing her gasp as she arched into him.

He liked that. Far too much. Moving to the other side, he repeated the action, loving the low moan she made, one hand coming off the bed to hold him against her.

"*Dios*, that feels so, so good."

He took his time, laying her back on the bed and kissing her. Shoulders, breasts, belly, before licking his way up to her chin. He took his time, swallowing each reaction, every sound she made.

"Tell me when you're ready, *querida*."

"Now, I'm ready now."

He kissed her mouth, tongue plunging in. She closed around him, and they remained like that for what seemed like an eternity, before he couldn't stand it any longer. Getting up, he kicked off his briefs, then sheathing himself and using the lubricant, he climbed back onto the bed and gently separated her thighs and levered himself on top of her, balancing on his forearms. Looking down at her, while trying his best to control his needs, he sought her eyes and looked into them. "Are you okay?"

"Yes. I'm more than okay."

The press of his pelvis against hers, the solid steadiness of his weight, was almost more than she could stand. He'd already built her up to a fever pitch that she hadn't felt since her accident.

She knew the second he entered her, not by feel, but by the way her back moved against the soft sheets.

Heaven. She was in heaven.

He set up a slow, steady pace, leaning down to whisper to her. Nonsensical things that had no meaning in and of themselves but added to the friction of his body against hers, the shivery need in the touch of his lips against her ear. It served as a pathway that connected her brain to her nerve endings.

That steady push and pull against her body was like waves of the ocean that tugged her back and then pushed her again to shore. It caused a spiraling need in her belly. Her nipples, every area of her body that could feel, and even those that could not, were being nudged toward something.

He wasn't asking her to do anything she couldn't do. He was helping her. Helping her feel. Helping her know that sex was still so very good.

Her arms wound around his neck after her fingernails trailed up his back in a soft scrape that was rewarded with a rough groan.

"What you do to me, *querida*."

What she did to him? Oh, man, what he was doing to her was the issue. He was be-witching her. Using some kind of sorcery to ratchet her to heights she hadn't achieved in a long, long time.

His rhythm changed and she used the muscles of her torso to move along with him, the scrape of the dusting of his chest hair over her nipples driving her crazy. Making her reach toward something.

She wanted…she wanted…

Dios! Some kind of lightning struck her, deleting her thoughts in an instant, until all there was, was a blast of sensation.

Her body couldn't be still, her arms tight-ening, head arching back into the pillow.

Santi gave a shout, the muscles in his neck straining under her fingers, and she knew he'd reached his own climax.

And heavens, it was every bit as good as it used to be when she could feel her orgasm. Every bit as fulfilling.

His body slowly relaxed against hers, lips nuzzling her neck in a way that tickled, making her giggle.

"You okay?"

"Mmm, sorry. Can't talk right now."

When he stiffened against her, she realized her words could have been taken more than one way, so she was quick to add, "Yes, I'm okay. Just trying to find my way back down that mountain. I—I'd forgotten just how good…"

A weird emotion went through her, and she had to stop talking.

Don't, Elle. God, please don't fall in love with him.

Why not? The voice whispered in the darkest recesses of her being. *You are worthy of love. Don't settle for anything less.*

Santi rolled off her and for a panicked second she thought he might try to pull her on top of him, but he didn't. He just lay there with his hands behind his head. He didn't say anything for a minute or two, then his hand touched hers and squeezed, causing her to relax and take a deep breath. Her muscles went slack with a deep sense of contentment. It was okay. There was no rejection here. She was safe.

Before she realized what was happening, her lids slid closed and that same sense of relaxation spread over her, causing blank spots in her brain that slowly moved to take over the parts that were responsible for thinking. When her muscles jerked, she realized she was falling asleep, and she made an effort to open her eyes again, finding him leaning over her.

He kissed her forehead. "Go to sleep. It's okay."

"You'll still be here when I wake up?"

There seemed to be a hesitation in his voice, but she was so drowsy and comfortable, she must have been mistaken, because the last thing she heard before unconsciousness took control of her was his deep voice.

"Yes. I'll be here."

CHAPTER TEN

Hours went by. Watching her sleep, Santi felt something kick him in the gut. A deep wrenching sense of guilt.

How often had he watched Carmen sleep just like this, unable to get enough of it? So many times. Times he could never get back again.

Carmen. He swallowed.

And now he was lapping this up like...

Diablos. There was no room for anyone else in his life. No room for another possibility of loss. This was why he didn't sleep with women on a regular basis. He'd always been afraid of finding himself in a spot just like this one: where emotions slid in and played games with his psyche, making him think things were possible that weren't.

He'd vowed he wasn't getting involved

with anyone ever again. The pain when Carmen had died had been debilitating. That was why he'd put his emotional energy into his work and volunteering rather than a relationship, not that he'd ever come this close to that familiar precipice.

And hell, he didn't want to go over it. Not again.

He needed to get out of here. But he'd promised her he would stay.

What an idiot. Sex was one thing. Making promises of any kind was another thing entirely.

But she looked so sweet. So totally at ease, all of her defenses lowered.

He had a feeling that more than one of his defenses had caved in as well, and he had to get home to rebuild them, before it was too late.

It's already too late.

Maldicion! Maybe it was. But that didn't mean he couldn't pull back and push Reset on everything. But in a way that wouldn't hurt her.

At least he hoped it wouldn't. Better to do it now than later, though.

And maybe it wasn't even an issue. Maybe

she wasn't interested in anything permanent, either. The other two women he'd been with hadn't been.

A murmur came from beside him and a hand reached out, touching the bed before finding his arm. Her eyes slowly slid open, squinting against the light that poured through the window, the warm brown of them threatening to do terrible things to his insides. He wanted to forget everything and roll over and spend another hour or two with her, drowning out his thoughts. His regrets.

But to do so would only make what he had to do harder.

Softening it with a smile, he pulled from her touch and hurriedly slid out of bed. Hauling on his briefs before facing her again, he tried to squelch the rush of desire that had poured over him. "I need to get back home. My housekeeper is used to my weird hours and will have taken care of Sasha, but it's not fair to leave her to do all of it while I…"

What could he say? While I fall in love? While I rip apart everything that was once Carmen's and hand it to someone else?

Elena pushed herself up with her arms,

the blankets falling to her waist, baring her torso.

Don't look.

He didn't, but he already knew every inch of her. It had somehow been burned into his brain.

Into his soul.

Her chin went up, but there was a suspicious tremble to her lower lip that told him he'd hurt her, despite everything. "I understand. I'll see you back at the hospital."

He sat on the bed and touched her cheek. "Elle, I want you to know—"

"Don't. I knew what this was when I invited you here. It's fine." She angled away from his touch. "But just so we're clear, this isn't going to happen again."

Those were the words he should have said. Instead, he'd been about to say something that would have put paid to all of his efforts to walk away.

Instead, Elena had saved him from himself. And for that he was grateful. He yanked on the rest of his clothes without looking back at her. Then his phone on the nightstand rang before he could get out of there. The ringtone said it was the hospital.

Then Elena's went off, too. A sense of foreboding went over him that had nothing to do with what had happened in that bed.

They both picked them up at the same time and answered.

Her eyes met his as he heard words he'd hoped not to hear.

It was Tomás. He'd taken a turn for the worse.

He hung up, and before he could say anything, she said, "Go. I'll meet you over there."

"Are you sure?"

A tiny thread of anger burned in her eyes. "I've been doing this for a very long time. I think I can manage without you."

The spear thrust deep and hit its mark. She was right. She had. And she would continue to long after the memories of last night had faded.

"I'll see you over there."

When Santi arrived at the hospital, rushing up to the third floor, he could hear Tomás's loud, pain-filled voice before he even got there. "They promised! They said I would be all right. That I wouldn't need a wheelchair."

He entered the room to find a nurse, trying to hold him in bed.

"Tomás, stop it." He laid his hand on the boy's shoulder, and he quieted almost immediately. "Tell me what's wrong."

"My legs. They have those pins and needles things, and this time it's not going away. And I can't feel my feet anymore. At all."

Hell. His surgery was supposed to be later today. "Lie back, so I can examine you."

Tears streaked the teen's face, and Santi knew what it had cost Tomás to let that emotion through. The sullenness of those first several meetings had given way to fear. The pain had to be unbearable. Santi didn't need to ask him what his pain levels were. He already knew. They were every bit as high as Santi's emotional pain was right now.

Being with Elle had brought everything roaring back, and the waves of it were still crashing over him despite leaving her house. And soon he would have to face her all over again.

Five minutes later, she wheeled into the room and took in the scene, her face showing nothing of the turmoil Santi was experiencing.

"His legs," she said.

"Yes. There's no sensation in his feet and the numbness is working its way up his legs."

"Did you call neuro?"

"Yes. Dr. Avario is en route now, and they're going to prep him for surgery now rather than wait."

"I agree." She wheeled over to the head of the bed, where Tomás was staring at the ceiling, his tears drying into white salty tracts, his face set in lines of resignation.

"You told me this wouldn't happen. That they could fix me." His voice was softer than Santi had ever heard it.

"They're going to take you to surgery as soon as Dr. Avario gets here. Your body is still growing and stretching your spinal cord. So we need to get it untethered."

"I can't feel my feet anymore. I can't even walk. I tried and fell."

"I know. I'm hoping surgery will return feeling to them."

His head turned on its pillow, fixing them both with a look that Santi would never forget. A quiet accusation that wound around him, squeezing the breath from him. "You promised. Just like all the others."

He had. He'd promised so many things.

To Tomás. To Carmen.

He couldn't make promises to anyone else. Not right now.

Where the hell was Avario?

Almost as if summoned, the man appeared in the doorway, his cool, unruffled manner in place, just as it always was.

"Well, young man, it sounds like we need to get you in and fix your back." He repeated the physical exam that Santi had just done, but it didn't bother him. He was the same way. He wanted to see for himself what the progression was.

He glanced at Santi. "Surgical suite prepped?"

"It's ready, there's a team waiting to get started."

Dr. Avario motioned him over to the side before asking, "Perfusionist?"

"Yes. He's ready in case you need to put him on bypass."

Tomás's Fontan circulation presented a big challenge for any type of surgery. And this one would be tricky, and it was hard to tell how long Tomás would need to be under anesthesia. Or exactly what they'd find once they got in there. Or if there would be more surgeries down the road.

"Okay, let's get him in there. Thanks for coming in." His gaze swept to include Elena. "Both of you. Without your diagnosis, we might not have found this in time."

Elena smiled, and there was still no sign of what had transpired in her bedroom before he left. "That's what I'm here for. Working on the hard cases."

Was that a reminder that he was one of the hardest cases yet? Or that she was here for the patients and not for him?

Well, of course she was. They hadn't even known who the other was when they met at Caitlin and Javier's wedding. At the time he'd been glad of that. Hadn't wanted to know her name.

Dios, that seemed like so long ago. But in reality it had been less than a month. A month in which so much had happened.

"What about Sasha?" Tomás was still looking daggers at him. "You said she'd be here when I got out of surgery."

Those daggers weren't nearly as sharp

as the ones he was using on himself. He'd been such a fool in so many ways. To think that he could walk away from Elle like he had the two women before her. Somehow this wasn't going to be nearly that easy. Or as painless.

"I know I did. And she will be. As soon as they wheel you out, I'm going to go pick her up and bring her back here."

It would give him a reason to get out of here and not have to face Elena's chilly silence.

Despite his best efforts, despite his saying she was in charge, he feared he'd broken that promise as well. In the end, he hadn't been able to be vulnerable and lay himself emotionally bare the way she had. Not once he'd come back to his senses.

He couldn't allow anything like that to happen again. Because he already knew a truth that his heart was keeping tucked in a quiet corner. Away from his mind. Away from anything that might try to crush it and stop it from growing.

In spite of all of his efforts and wrangling and arguments. He'd fallen in love. Again. And Santi had no idea what to do about it.

* * *

While Santi went to pick up his dog, Elena hurriedly packed up the stuff in her temporary office.

Temporary. Just like last night with Santi had been.

She ached in a way that had nothing to do with a physical sense of pain, but something that was lodged deep inside her. If she didn't deal with it, it would fester and turn something that had been beautifully fulfilling into something dark and ugly. Something like she'd experienced with Renato years ago.

It could turn her bitter.

But only if she let it.

Instead, she needed to accept it for what it was. A one-night stand that had blown her expectations out of the water.

She slumped in her chair for a moment as a wave of anguish went through her. Why did it have to be Santi who awoke those feelings in her? Why not some random man in some random place. Other than her bed.

She frowned. Except Santi was some random man. Wasn't he?

No. He was a man who was still in love with his dead wife. She'd seen it in his eyes as she'd reached for him. He'd almost re-coiled away. And the sadness and fear she'd seen in him had crushed any hope she might have of a meaningful relationship with him.

Was that what she'd expected when she invited him home? Despite her words to the contrary?

She didn't know. All she knew was he hadn't been able to get away from her fast enough when they'd been prepping for Tomás's surgery. She knew he had to get Sasha, but his attitude matched what she'd seen in her apartment. He didn't want to be near her. And she shouldn't want to be near him.

Because right now her emotions were so tangled up that she couldn't separate truth from fantasy.

And that's what their encounter had been right? A fantasy? One where the handsome prince carried her over the threshold and promised to love her forever? Or rode off into the sunset to live happily ever after.

Santi had already had that happy ending with one person and it looked like he wasn't going to be able to have it with anyone else besides his late wife.

So she would just put that from her mind and pull herself back to reality.

With that in mind, she finished putting her laptop in her bag and the few other items she'd accumulated onto her desk. It would take her a few trips to get things up there. But from what Dr. Avario had said, surgery would take a couple of hours at least. She dreaded seeing Santi again. But that was the reality of it. She was going to have to see him. For as long as she remained at Aelina.

What if she didn't stay? What if she went back to rotating from hospital to hospital? Or went back to the island where she grew up.

Yes, running looked very attractive right now. Too attractive.

She wasn't going to make any decisions now, though. Not until she'd had time to sit back and think about everything that had happened. To decide if she could move past it, or if it was going to continually cause her pain.

But for now, she would do what she had to do to keep functioning. And that began with removing herself from his realm.

With that, she headed for the elevator with her first load of items. Pressing the button for the fifth floor, and watching the doors as they closed, she felt like she was also closing the door on that episode in her bedroom and entering a new space mentally. One that she hoped was devoid of anything involving the handsome pediatrician. If that didn't help, then she was going to make a decision every bit as hard as the one she'd made when she quit trying to regain the use of her legs. She would turn the page on this chapter and start her story all over again. A story that had no place for Santi or the idea of a forever love.

An hour later, Elena was in a waiting room. One where Santi and Sasha sat a few feet from her. Neither of them said much, although she greeted Sasha with a quick hug. Santi was right to have picked up the pup. Right now, Tomás and his well-being were far more important than heart-to-heart conversations or talks about where she and Santi went from here.

She said nothing about clearing out her office. And if she was honest with herself, she didn't think she could bear to see the relief in Santi's eyes when he found out she was no longer housed on the third floor. She only hoped she would be long out of sight when he realized. But right now, all she was going to do was think about Tomás. At least that was her hope.

Dios. She hoped the teen regained use of his legs. It would be agonizing for him to have to face one more crisis in his life after he'd suffered so much already.

Letizia came in, saving her from sitting in awkward silence. "How's he doing?"

"No word yet, but it's only been an hour."

"That is one brave kid."

Elle lifted a shoulder. "I think he's one scared kid. He doesn't have a choice of whether to be brave or not. And he certainly doesn't deserve this."

"Do any of us deserve the suffering we go through?"

She was keenly aware that her friend had parked herself to include Santi in the conversation.

Santi was someone else who had endured something no one deserved to go through. His wife had suffered and died. And she was pretty sure a piece of Santi had died with her. Like the part of his heart that might have allowed him to fall in love again. Or to have a relationship like the one he'd had with his late wife. If so, she couldn't imagine anything sadder. Her brief relationship with her professor had soured her, but it hadn't killed anything inside her. Maybe that wasn't so with Santi.

Last night certainly seemed to bear that out. Not that she thought she'd be the one to prove to him that life could still be good after surviving a trauma like that. But she hoped he could find someone who could.

Her heart cramped at the thought of him with someone else. With anyone else.

Not good, Elle. Not good.

"No. No one deserves to suffer," she murmured. "But I hope Tomás can get through this. Not only that. I hope he can get his own family. One who won't return him, saying that the challenge of having him in their home was too much for them."

Like her finding someone who didn't think the challenges of loving her were too much for them?

"I've been thinking about Tomás. A lot."

Elena hadn't been aware that her friend knew that much about the teen. But there was something in her eyes.

"You have?"

Santi hadn't said anything, but she could tell he was listening to every word Letizia said.

"He deserves a better chance than the one he's getting." Her friend clasped her hands in her lap. "I'm thinking of applying to be a foster parent. Actually, I've been toying with the idea for a long time. Every time the group home brings a kid to the hospital, my mind returns there. Would either of you be willing to serve as a reference, if I decide to move forward?"

This was why she'd come down to sit with them. A prickling began deep in her eyes and radiated outward. "Of course I will. I'd be honored, Leti."

"I would, too."

The deep baritone tones came from beside her, causing that wrenching sensation in her heart to happen all over again. So he'd serve as a reference as long as he didn't have to commit his heart.

Stop it!

"Thank you both." Her mentor looked from one to the other. "Do you mind if I sit here with you until Tomás is out of surgery?"

"Of course not." It would be a relief actually to have a buffer. To have someone who could keep hard subjects from coming up. Who could keep Santi from trying to issue another awful apology that cut deeper than any scalpel known to man.

And who could keep her from thinking or saying things she might someday come to regret.

Like *I love you*?

Oh, God. Please, no. Please don't fall in love with a man who seems incapable of loving you back.

That voice was inside her, whispering that it was already too late. That the care and sensual way he'd made love to her last night had caused her to hope for something she'd long thought was beyond her reach. Like riding Strato.

But was it? She'd seen firsthand at On Horses' Wings that it wasn't out of the realm of possibility. It was just her fear that had allowed her to believe it was.

Maybe it was easier that way. Easier not to hope for something that might cause disappointment or anguish.

She glanced over at Santi to see that he

was reading something on his phone. And she was shocked to realize his proud profile was already burned into her brain.

The man was the whole package. He loved his work. Loved the kids he worked with. Loved his dog.

The only thing he didn't love, evidently, was her.

Those words turned over and over in her head until she couldn't stand it anymore. "I'm going to get some coffee. Does anyone else want some?"

"Nothing for me," said Letizia.

"A coffee sounds great. But I can get them."

"Nope, I need to move, so I'll go. How do you want it?"

Too late she realized that last question could be misconstrued. It was there in the narrowing of his eyes. In the way his fingers tightened on his phone.

"Black."

"Okay." He liked his coffee unadorned. Like his life? Devoid of anything that might add flavor or color to it?

Diablos. She was reading way too much into everything.

When he tried to hand her money, she shook her head. "I have a machine that uses pods in my office. I'll just make the coffees there."

Except she'd forgotten that she'd already packed her office up and hauled her stuff to the fifth floor. She hadn't set her coffee machine up yet. But she wasn't about to retract her words. So she wheeled down to the cafeteria and picked up two coffees. Hers a skinny vanilla latte and his a dark, opaque brew that made her shiver. Light didn't always vanquish the night. Her optimism on most days couldn't always erase someone else's pain, and it shouldn't. But, oh, how she wished it could.

What she did know, however, was that she couldn't let whatever dark currents that swirled inside Santi quench the joy she'd found in living life to the fullest.

Even if it meant steering clear of him now and for the rest of her life.

CHAPTER ELEVEN

HER OFFICE HAD been cleared out.

He'd gone to see her when Letizia had contacted him again for a reference after their talk yesterday.

A moment of panic went through him, and he pulled out the chair she'd replaced under the desk and sat in it for a minute. As far as he knew she'd been in here yesterday. She'd certainly stayed in the waiting room for the rest of the time, until they'd gotten word on Tomás.

Had she lied to him about staying at Aelina? Had his attitude done something to make her decide to leave the hospital?

It made him think of the professor from her past who had treated her with such insensitivity.

And really, had Santi done any better by her?

Probably not. His head hadn't been in the best of places after waking up in her bed. It still wasn't. There was a lot of junk in there that needed to be separated and sorted, but he just didn't have the emotional energy or desire to do it right now.

And if he never did?

Honestly, it might be easier if he didn't. Life had moved along pretty damn smoothly for the last couple of years. Until Elle had come along and made him feel things he hadn't felt in a very long time. Hadn't *wanted* to feel in a very long time.

Tomás had come out of surgery with flying colors and as soon as he woke up, he said the pain in his legs was gone. And his toes and feet were tingling in a way that said the nerve endings were reviving. He hadn't needed to go on bypass, which was another good thing.

And he'd been so happy to see Sasha when he woke up. Said that she was good luck for him.

He didn't know about good luck, but Letizia seemed to be following through with what she'd said in the waiting room. And if it panned out, that boy would be with one of the best, most competent people he knew. And she had a dog of her own. A big Labradoodle that would be the answer to his desire to have a dog. The stars certainly seemed to be lining up in the teen's favor. Finally.

If only they could line up that way for him.

He decided to call Letizia under the guise of telling her he'd received the document and see if she volunteered any information on Elena.

Maldizion! If he'd somehow hurt her…

Before he could, however, his phone rang, sending his heart into overdrive. When he looked at the readout, however, he saw that the caller was Grace.

"Hello?"

"Hi, Santi. It's Grace."

Despite his earlier thoughts, he smiled. "I can see that from my caller ID."

"Smart ass! I hadn't heard back from you about my and Diego's renewal ceremony on Friday and wanted to make sure you were coming."

Hell, he'd totally forgotten about that. "Sorry. It slipped my mind. Of course I'll be there."

He could have made up an excuse, but Grace was pretty intuitive. She'd know if he were lying. But right now, the last thing he wanted to go through was witnessing yet another set of vows.

You're not "going through" anything. This is about Grace and Diego. Not you.

"Great. Do you want me to seat you and Elena together?"

His brain froze for a few seconds before he was able to figure out an answer. "Why would you do that?"

"Uh… I don't know. I thought maybe…" There was a pause. "Never mind. Forget I asked that."

"Okay. I didn't realize seats were assigned."

"They're not really, but we're not having a huge contingent of guests, so I was trying to organize things a bit. But that's probably not a good idea. Sit wherever you'd like. Gotta go. See you Friday, if not before."

"Sounds good."

With that the line went dead, leaving him to wonder if Elena had told her about what happened between them. The women seemed to have become friends, but hell, he didn't want their night together making the rounds.

He could call the diagnostician and ask her outright, but right now he didn't want to hear her voice. Didn't want to ask her if she was still at Aelina or if she were out of his life forever.

His chest constricted until it was hard to breathe.

So he called Letizia, like he'd planned to do.

She answered on the first ring. "Hi, Santi. I take it you got the request for a reference form. Did you change your mind?"

"About?"

"About giving me a reference. What else would I mean?"

"Nothing." He needed to get more rest or something. He hadn't felt himself since sleeping with Elena, and he didn't know why.

Well… He knew. He just didn't want to examine the reasons or do anything about them. Even if he'd gotten emotionally entangled with her, it didn't mean he had to act on it or allow it to drag him to the bottom of that particular pool. Maybe it would even be easier if she really had moved on to another place of employment. Out of sight, out of mind, wasn't that what they said?

Except, that hadn't been true about Carmen, had it? And he had a feeling it wouldn't be true of Elena, either.

What a huge, huge mess he'd made. Of everything.

"Are you okay, Santi?"

"Yes, why wouldn't I be?"

"I don't know, you just seemed out of sorts yesterday in the waiting room."

He knew he had. He'd caught several of Elena's sideways glances. He'd pretended to be enthralled by something on his phone. Which was a big fat nothing. His screen had been blank. Just like the screen on his heart. For six long years it had been a dark hole that he'd stared down into instead of looking up at the life going on around him.

"I was just worried about Tomás." He needed to bring up Elena's empty office but had no idea how to word it without giving her some of the same ideas that Grace evidently had.

"I know you were. I bet it's a lot quieter down in pediatrics since Elena left."

His whole being seemed to ice over, making it hard to move his lips. "She left?"

"Of course. You didn't know? Her office down there was only temporary, remember? She's up on the fifth floor now. I'm surprised she didn't say something."

The sense of relief came out of nowhere, weighing him down and pinning him in place. "I didn't. But yes, I did remember her permanent office was going to be up there."

With Dario. The flirt.

The fact that a move to the fifth floor hadn't been what had popped into his head when he'd first arrived to find her gone was telling. He expected the worst out of situations many times, even though he'd denied it time and time again to those who cared about him. This was another of those cases, where he'd assumed the worst, even when it hadn't happened.

But her leaving wouldn't be the worst thing. Wasn't that what he'd just finished convincing himself of?

Maybe she'd even be better off with someone like Dario than with him.

"So the reference. You're going to fill it out for me? I've spoken to the group home's director and told her I was going to apply for guardianship of Tomás at the very least, but I asked her to keep it between us for the moment. I don't want to get his hopes up, just to have them crushed if my application isn't approved."

"Anyone who knows you knows how competent you are. In every area. I can't imagine this being any different."

"Thanks, Santi. *De tus labios a los oídos de Dios.*"

From his lips to God's ears. That saying was pretty ironic, since his lips had murmured prayers during Carmen's sickness that had never seemed to reach the ears of any deity. But that hadn't meant he hadn't tried. Time and time again, only to be met with stony silence. And suffering. And, in the end, death.

"I wouldn't count on me for that, Letizia."

After a few more minutes of conversation involving Tomás and the medical needs and challenges the boy had, they said goodbye. And Santi found himself murmuring the first quiet words to God that he'd uttered in over six years. And this time, it wasn't for himself or for Carmen. Or for Elena. It was for a teenage boy who'd gotten so few breaks in his life.

He and Carmen had at least had three years of happiness before her death. And if she were up there looking down at him, she probably wasn't thrilled with what she saw of his life. His days had been spent working harder than he should. And of being far less happy than most people were.

And yet, what could he do about it?

Maybe for a start he could go to Grace and Diego's vow renewal ceremony and be genuinely happy for them, rather than wallowing in his own self-pity. He could start looking outside and enjoying some sunrises and spend his jogging time being thankful for the good things in his life.

Like Elena?

No, she wasn't in his life in a real way. Maybe because he hadn't allowed her to be. But what he did know was that he wasn't going to impulsively jump into something that might bring both of them grief. What if they weren't compatible?

From what he'd seen, he didn't think that was a real issue. But he couldn't afford to hurt her by trying to move on from Carmen and failing. So what he had to do was spend some time really thinking about what he wanted and didn't want out of life.

And then he needed to act, or he needed to put it out of his mind and his heart. Once and for all.

"Hey, you." Grace popped her head around the door of Elena's office. "Are you busy?"

"Not right now, come in." The truth was, she hadn't been nearly as busy as she'd expected to be, and it gave her far too much time to think and mope around about things she couldn't change.

Grace dropped into one of the chairs. "I meant to come by yesterday after talking to Santi but got too busy."

She'd spoken to Santi? About what?

"Okay…"

"I wanted to make sure our plans to make the ceremony accessible are on target. We're planning to construct a kind of wooden boardwalk that goes from the parking area across the beach and widens as it goes between the rows of seating, so that wheelchairs can park next to the seats without hindering the flow of traffic."

Elena smiled. "That sounds perfect. Thank you for doing that. I would have made it to the ceremony even if I had to stay on the asphalt of the parking area."

"That would make me incredibly sad. I want you there with everyone else." She hesitated. "Speaking of which, I asked Santi if he wanted me to seat you together, and he got kind of weirded out. I'm sorry if I stepped out of line. I don't want to pry, I just thought you guys were getting along really well. I'd even hoped…"

Grace's brows went up in question and Elena shook her head.

"I actually did, too. But you know, love is one of those things I've never been able to figure out."

She and Grace stared at each other for a long minute as she realized she'd let the cat out of the bag. But keeping that word to herself had been killing her over the last couple of days.

Grace reached across and grabbed her hand. "Give him a chance, Elle. Santi has fought against his feelings for so long that, well…" She took a visible breath. "After Carmen died, we were all worried about him. Really worried. We even thought he might have a breakdown of some sort. He shut off his feelings just like a water spigot. He threw himself into work, but he wasn't the same."

"You don't have to—"

"I want you to understand. He's not fighting you. He's in a battle against himself. If he'd gone to counseling like so many of us advised, he might have been able to accept the idea of falling in love and remarrying, but as it is…" Grace tipped up a shoulder. "I guess I can understand to a certain extent. When Diego and I fell in love I tried to tell myself it wasn't happening. That it couldn't happen. Not to me. Not when I'd fought so hard not to be one of those statistics. But you can't always choose who you love, or when. That's why I said to give him a chance. He might just need some time to figure it all out."

"And if he doesn't? I don't think I can stand to stay at Aelina if I have to see him day in and day out."

"Please don't tell me you're thinking of leaving."

She realized she had been. The idea had

sprung up out of the ashes of their night together, and she'd been unconsciously watering it. Right now the stalk and first leaves were growing steadily and pretty soon she'd be forced to make a decision.

"I haven't decided anything yet."

"I'm so sorry for making things worse."

She squeezed her friend's hand before releasing it. "You haven't. In fact, maybe you've helped me face some pretty hard truths. And maybe Santi, too."

"Face them, yes. But don't make any hard-and-fast decisions while you're in pain. If I'd done that, Diego and I would probably be going our own separate ways. Just give it a few weeks. Or maybe even a few months. I promise everything will become clear in time. Don't make a decision about forever that you may come to regret. Promise?"

She nodded. "I promise." She forced a smile. "And thanks. For the ramp. And… for everything."

"That's what friends are for, *querida*." With that, Grace rose to her feet. "I'll see you on Friday."

"Okay, see you there." As soon as she said it, she realized that her avoidance tactics were doomed to fail. Despite moving to the fifth floor and doing her best to not stop on the third floor for anything, she and Santi were bound to run into each other from time to time. The renewal ceremony was proof of that.

All she could do was go and see how she felt. She wheeled herself around to face the large picture window behind her desk and looked out over the city of Barcelona. The sun was a mere speck on the horizon, red shafts of light painting the clouds and the city beneath it with a glorious glow. As she sat there thinking about all that had happened since she'd moved there these last couple of weeks, lights began flickering on, one by one all across the area. The beauty in that was unmistakable. Building after building, street after street became illuminated against the deepening shadows. And she couldn't help but hope that a light very much like these would pop on in Santi's head and banish his own darkness. And that he would realize that life wasn't over for him. He could find happiness and a whole new beginning, if only he'd allow himself to.

And if he couldn't?

Then she was going to have a very hard decision to make. Grace was right. She didn't have to make it right now. But she also couldn't put off the inevitable forever.

Friday came far too soon. Hell, he'd been stupid to nix Grace's idea of seating him and Elena together. Maybe it would have forced him to muster up the courage to talk to her. As it was, he hadn't caught sight of her since the day of Tomás's surgery almost a week ago.

It was almost as if she were avoiding him.

Like he was avoiding her?

Of course she was. He hadn't given her any reason to do otherwise.

He walked down the boardwalk, his thoughts again on Carmen. The truth of how unhappy she'd be with how he was dealing with her loss had been weighing on his mind more and more. It was a hard realization to come to. He'd been given the wonderful opportunity of a second chance, and he'd been willing to throw it all away, all over a misguided sense of guilt.

Would he have wanted Carmen to do the same if their situations had been reversed?

Hell no. He would have found a way to haunt her for the rest of her life if she had.

There were so many coincidences attached to his and Elena's first and second meetings that it made him wonder if the diagnostician had somehow been sent to him. Maybe his prayers hadn't been completely unheard after all. They just hadn't been answered in the way he'd expected them to be.

On impulse, he'd made a weird purchase yesterday on a rare trip into Barcelona, surprised when he'd seen the item in a storefront window.

Coincidences. It was what finally made him decide to face whatever it was he felt for Elena head-on. He was going to do it after the ceremony. If she even came.

The waves lapped against the shore in front of them and the scent of salt on the breeze was thick and warm and bracing. He breathed it in, glad to be alive in a way he hadn't been for a long time. He dragged his hand through his hair and found a seat near the back just off the boardwalk.

Where Elle could see him? Probably.

He'd arrived twenty minutes before the

ceremony, maybe unconsciously hoping to find her and pull her his way.

And if she rejected him? Hell, he couldn't blame her if she did. He'd certainly rejected her. The look on her face after she'd reached for him only to have him step away had haunted him. If he was right, she cared for him, or at least she had in that moment.

And now?

Demonio. He was so confused about his own feelings that he hadn't really stopped to think about what he might have done to her, beyond the superficial worry about hurting her.

What if he'd done permanent damage, the way that goon of a professor had? What if it stayed with her for years?

What if she went out with Dario and he did the same?

He swallowed. Yes, whether or not they were able to work this out, he needed to talk to her and set the record straight. Those stupid words "It's not you, it's me" were all too true in this case. It had been wholly about him and had nothing to do with what he'd been beginning to feel for her.

Diego came alongside him, stopping to

shake his hand and give him a lopsided grin. The Spaniard looked cool and confident in light khakis and a loose shirt, a perfect combination for the beach, which is what Grace had asked her guests to wear.

Santi had opted for dark jeans and a white linen shirt with rolled-up sleeves. He hoped it met with Grace's approval.

"Have you seen my bride yet?"

"Not yet." The man didn't look worried about being stood up; it was more of a simple question. Or maybe he was just anxious to get this show on the road. "And congratulations. I'm glad things worked out for you two."

"Me, too. I'm just glad I didn't blow my chances with her."

Grace glided up to meet them in a loose white dress that floated just above her knees, revealing tanned legs and sandals that looked to have a million crisscrossed straps. She smiled. "You didn't." She didn't ask what they were talking about, seeming to already know.

Maybe that's what love was.

He and Carmen had had that. And so had he and Elle that day at the estate where Caitlin and Javier's wedding had been. Coincidence? He was beginning to think more and more that it hadn't been. He just hadn't recognized it at the time. And now?

Yes, he thought he finally did. And like Diego, he hoped it wasn't too late.

Diego bent to kiss her. "Are you ready to make this official?"

"It already is, silly. We're just telling the world we're sticking with each other. I'm glad Caitlin and her new hubby made it back in time for the ceremony."

Santi spotted the pair on the other side of the aisle. Javier's arm was around Caitlin's shoulders and the pair looked relaxed and very much in love. There were a couple of other faces he recognized. Diego's sister Isabella was there with Carlos Martinez. The couple was expecting their first child in about four months.

It seemed love was definitely in the air.

Diego made his way to the front, where his best man and the hospital's minister were waiting. Grace turned back and hovered at the start of the aisle, waiting for the violins to cue her walk to the front. Santi caught a flurry of movement behind him and turned to see Grace laughing as she hugged an older woman before the music started up and they walked arm in arm to where Diego was waiting.

All of the pair's family and friends were there, with very few chairs left open. Except for Elle, who still hadn't made it.

Maybe she wasn't coming. What if she'd decided to leave Aelina after all, the way he'd feared on Monday when he found her office vacated.

What was he going to do if that were the case?

He would do what he should have done a week ago. He was going to hunt her down and talk to her. Tell her what he'd discovered about himself and ask her if she felt the same way.

Dios! And if she didn't? Or if unlike Diego, he really had screwed up his chances with her?

Well, at least he'd know he'd tried and not buried his head in the sand and attempted to pretend life would move on by, unseen and unfelt. Except life around him was pretty dull and gray, despite the beauty of today's setting. And he realized it was all due to Elena's absence.

Hand in hand, Diego and Grace renewed their vows, their eyes never leaving each other. And the farther into the service they got, the more uneasy he felt about his own prospects. It wasn't like Elena to be late for anything. She was one of the most organized people he'd ever met. It was one of the reasons she was so good at what she did.

Just as he was thinking about getting up in the middle of the ceremony and going to find her, she appeared beside him, stopping her chair and setting the brake.

He swallowed back a huge ball of emotion, letting go of the fear he'd felt moments earlier that he'd lost her completely.

She wouldn't have chosen to sit beside him if that were the case, would she?

Man, he didn't deserve her. Didn't deserve a second chance to be with her, but here it was, as if handed to him. He wasn't going to turn his back on it again.

He leaned closer. "I was afraid you weren't going to come."

"Tomás wanted to speak with me. That's why I'm late."

She didn't seem angry or upset. She just seemed like... Elle. The one he'd grown to know and love.

He frowned. "All okay?"

"He's fine. I'll tell you about it once the ceremony is done."

Elle's hand was resting on the arm of her chair, and before he could stop himself, he covered it with his own, entwining his fingers with hers. He waited for her to pull away or make some sign that she didn't want this. Or him.

Instead she seemed to sigh, her digits closing around his own. Her eyes met his and a sort of silent communication passed between them before they turned their attention back to the front.

A sense of hope rose in his chest, as his heart grew lighter and lighter with each moment that passed. And when Diego pulled Grace into an embrace and kissed her with a fervor that was unmistakable, he tightened his grip until he was sure Elle would notice. And she did. But she didn't ask him to release her. Instead she laid her right hand over their joined ones and whispered, "I know."

He believed it. If Grace had been able to read him so easily, then why wouldn't Elena?

The couple at the front finally broke apart to much laughter as Grace's hand went to cover her heart and she then put her palm to Diego's lips. Then they turned to face their loved ones, hands raised high in the air for all to see. This was one union that was going to stand the test of time. The way he hoped his and Elena's one day would.

As the happy couple made their way back down the walkway, Grace found Santi's eyes and gave him a wink and a quick thumbs-up. Then they were gone, off to a reception before sweeping away to their long-overdue honeymoon.

As the guests began to make their way down the aisle heading toward the festivities, Santi and Elena stayed where they were, until they were the only ones left on the sand.

"Tomás is okay?"

"He's doing great. He told me that Letizia broke the news that she's trying to become his foster parent and that they've been spending a lot of time getting to know each other this week."

He smiled. "She told me she was going to try to wait to tell him until things were more certain."

"Evidently they are. Tomás has been so unhappy at the group home that the director petitioned the courts to fast-track Letizia's application, and the process is very nearly finished. No one sees any reason why it can't or shouldn't happen."

"That's wonderful."

"Yes."

They sat there in silence for a few seconds before they both tried to speak. They laughed and then Elena told him to go ahead.

"I need to apologize for something—" He stopped at her stricken look and then realized what she thought he was going to say. "No. Not for what happened that night between us, but for my behavior afterward. I felt things I hadn't felt in a very long time, and frankly, it scared the hell out of me."

"I know. Me, too."

He lifted her hand and kissed it. "I'm sorry for walking out like I did. It was cowardly, and I hope you can forgive me. Because I love you."

"And Carmen?"

He frowned. "What about her?"

He hoped she wasn't going to ask him to compare them because he couldn't. He couldn't explain how he could love his late wife and still feel this piercing, uncontrollable love for the woman seated next to him. The one he hoped felt the same thing for him. But it was there. And he wasn't going to deny it any longer.

"Grace told me a little bit about what happened after her death. I know I'm not her but—"

"I know you're not. And I love *you*. Not because you're anything like her. You're not. And that's a good thing, Elle. You're not someone to take her place. You're someone I love because… Well, I just can't stop myself. Believe me, I tried. It's there, despite every effort I've made to stop it from happening."

She laughed. "That describes what's happened to me in a nutshell. You make me happy. That's all there is to it. And the thought of you not feeling the same way was gutting. I love you, too, Santi. I love the way you try your best to help your patients, the way you give to kids at the center. The way you love horses. And your reaction to that silly painting at the Maravilla estate."

He tipped her chin and looked into her eyes. "Do you believe in coincidences?"

"What?"

"I need to show you something. Will you come with me?"

"Where?"

"Back to my house." He grinned. "I rode my bike here, though, so…"

"I'll drive. I'm right back there in the parking lot."

He drew a deep breath, the crush of the past finally beginning to loosen its grip. He kissed her. Softly. Deeply. Trying to infuse everything he felt for her into that act.

They loaded his bike into the van and Santi told her how to get to his house. They stopped outside and she stared at the white stucco house with his clay-tiled roof. "Your home is beautiful."

He tried to see it through her eyes, but all he saw was the house he'd lived in for the last six years. And he realized he'd never made it a home. Not really. But he hoped that was going to change very soon.

He opened the door, and he called out to

Maria, his housekeeper, who was following Sasha as she rushed to greet him. After a few yips and turning circles of happiness, the dog turned her attention to Elle, whom she also greeted just as enthusiastically. Then Santi smiled at Maria.

"This is Elena Solis. She's my..." His words trailed away as he realized they hadn't made anything official. Fortunately, his housekeeper saved him from his blunder.

"I already know," she said. "I've been hoping to meet you."

Hell, did everyone know what he felt before he did? Probably. He'd just been too stubborn to let his heart tell his brain what was what. At least until now.

Maria went on, "I have some things to do in my cottage, so if you'll excuse me."

She turned and exited the room.

Elle looked at him. "Does that seem weird to you? Grace came to my office this past week and already knew that I was in love with you."

"I was just thinking the same thing. Like I said, there are so many coincidences about us that it makes me think...never mind." He wasn't going to say that he wondered if Carmen had ordered God to send him someone to love. He didn't want to ruin what was happening here. "Which brings up what I was going to show you. I happened to be walking past an art gallery and saw something."

Santi drew her into the next room, Sasha hard on their heels. In the drawing room was a framed print, facing the wall. Elle looked at it, her head tilted. "What is that?"

"It's one of the biggest coincidences of all. And I can tell you that I finally understand its meaning."

He went over to the painting and slowly turned it around to face her.

Elle's hand went to her mouth. "That was at an art gallery?"

"It's not the original, of course, but it's a print of the original."

The framed image was a replica of the one that hung on the wall at the Maravilla estate. It was a man and a woman sitting sidesaddle on a horse that was racing across the countryside.

"Wow. I don't know what to say."

He set the picture against the wall as he watched her study it. "I hoped it might help 'sell' me to you."

"You don't need to sell yourself to me. That auction ended the moment I watched your head tilt in confusion at that painting."

"Me, too. I just didn't realize it at the time." He glanced at the print. "I'd like to hang that in our bedroom, if you're in agreement."

"*Our* bedroom?"

"Is that so hard to imagine?"

She shook her head, her hand buried in Sasha's fur. "No. Actually it's not. It's like a dream. Something so unimaginable that I'm having trouble believing it."

"Kind of like that painting?"

"Yes, it's exactly like that painting. And having a reminder is a good thing. To remember that what might seem impossible is actually very possible. Especially when you're talking about love."

"De tus labios a los oídos de Dios." He found himself repeating the words that Letizia had said to him over the phone less than a week ago. From your lips to God's ears. The prayers he once thought went unanswered hadn't been. And he was so very grateful.

"Let's change that to from *our* lips to

God's ears. Because we're in this together, Santi. You and me. And I wouldn't have it any other way."

"Me, either, sweetheart. Me, either."

EPILOGUE

Six months later

STRATO AND BILLY stood side by side in the arena of On Horses' Wings. The place had been transformed into a garden oasis with draped lighting, and flowers and plants of every kind imaginable.

Elena could barely believe this was possible. And if Santi hadn't thought it was, he never would have let this happen. The horse that had once stood over her, trying to make sure she was okay after her accident, had been sent to a trainer who specialized in equines whose owners were differently abled.

He told her Strato had taken to the training so easily, it was almost as if he'd been waiting for this his whole life. And maybe he had been. The man's words had made her cry, partly for all the time she'd wasted but mostly for the opportunity to sit astride her beautiful horse once again.

She glanced at Santi, wondering if he was thinking the same thing. That the very thing that had helped her sit her horse had given her an idea of ways she could sit on him with a little extra support.

The results had been…very, very satisfying, for them both.

When he winked at her, her face heated.

Seated in chairs that had been draped in white fabric were both sets of parents and family and friends. Sandra was her maid of honor and stood next to Strato, holding a bouquet of red roses. Every once in a while her horse eyed that bouquet in a way that made her smile. He still had a mischievous streak to him, but when it came to riding, he'd learned to listen to her hand cues rather than those from her legs.

And Santi's best "man" was Tomás, who had been officially adopted by Letizia last week and was doing so very well. It was meant to be, they all agreed.

Just like her and Santi.

When she'd asked him if they could be married at the center on their horses rather than at some beautiful but unfamiliar venue, he'd agreed instantly. And On Horse's Wings became the place of her dreams.

They gripped hands as their horses stood in the midst of loved ones, and when Santi stood in his stirrups and leaned over to kiss her, she shivered. There was nowhere she'd rather be than with this man and these two horses.

She was now volunteering at the center as well, learning a different way to interact and care for the animals she loved so much.

The flash of a phone's camera made Strato snort for a second, but he stood stone-still as if he were carrying a piece of porcelain. The way Santi had carried her to bed that first time. And she understood. It wasn't because they were afraid of hurting her, although that might have been part of it, but because they cared about her.

And she was grateful. Grateful for Santi. Grateful for her work. Grateful for life.

And full of more love than she ever thought possible.

When the minister invited them to kiss once again, they did. With the promise of a bright future and the hope that forever truly was possible.

* * * * *

If you missed the previous story in the Night Shift in Barcelona quartet, then check out

Their Marriage Worth Fighting For
by Louisa Heaton

And if you enjoyed this story, check out these other great reads from Tina Beckett

One Night with the Sicilian Surgeon
Their Reunion to Remember
Starting Over with the Single Dad

All available now!